THE GREENBRIER GHOST III

FEATURING STORIES ABOUT THE

BRAXTON COUNTY GREEN MONSTER

THE GREENBRIER GHOST III

FEATURING STORIES ABOUT THE

BRAXTON COUNTY GREEN MONSTER

By Dennis Deitz

Mountain Memories Books

Mountain Memories Books
Charleston, WV

10 9 8 7 6 5 4 3 2 1

Printed in West Virginia

Library of Congress Catalog Number: 2003100009

ISBN 0-938985-01-9

© 2003 Dennis Deitz
All Rights Reserved

Distributed by:
Pictorial Histories Distribution
1416 Quarrier Street
Charleston, WV 25301
wvbooks@ntelos.net

ACKNOWLEDGEMENTS

Thank you to the many people who gave me stories, my loyal readers who have encouraged me, and Bob Bush who took the pictures and helped with the interviews. Also a special "thanks" to Sandy Underwood from The Printing Press.

FOREWORD

Dennis Deitz, the 88 year old South Charleston author, is about to present us with another treat to enjoy reading: "Greenbrier Ghost #3". This book differs from "Greenbrier Ghost #1" and "Greenbrier Ghost #2" in that it does not merely deal with ghost stories. "Greenbrier Ghost #3" (although it is not about the "Greenbrier Ghost") continues as a collection of stories that are sometimes heartwarming, and sometimes eerie, but always interesting. These stories were told to Mr. Deitz by folks he has met and interviewed. According to their recollections, these accounts are factual.

Mr. Deitz himself had an interesting beginning. He was born on September 27, 1913. Because a fire had destroyed the main house on the family farm, the family had temporarily moved into the chicken house. He was born in that chicken house. The farm is located between Drunkard's Roost and Squat' n Dodge, Greenbrier County, West Virginia. Is it any wonder he has been able to locate people with interesting and different tales to tell ? He has a few he himself can tell!

Although Mr. Deitz has written on a wide range of subjects, he did not begin his writing career until he was 70. He started with "Mountain Memories 1", a collection of old stories people would hand down through generations as told to him by his brother, Granville Deitz. This book is an example of true stories that were enhanced by people as they were retold over and over again through the years. There seemed to be so much interest in "Mountain Memories 1", that Deitz wrote a second, a third and eventually five "Mountain Memories" books. These books all deal with stories about how families lived in the mountains of West Virginia in the early part of the 20th century. Some stories are about Mr. Deitz' family and some stories were told to him by others. In all these books, Mr. Deitz tried to preserve stories about people and events and the way they lived for future generations. Even today, that way of life seems so foreign to young people. Mr. Deitz gets great pleasure in visiting area schools and sharing his experiences with students.

Among his other writings are two books on tragic floods in West Virginia. "The Flood and the Blood" deals with the 1916 and the

1932 floods that occurred in Paint Creek and in Cabin Creek. The sad and terrifying tales as told by the survivors brings to life that horrible event. "Buffalo Creek, Valley of Death" deals with the Buffalo Creek flood. When an earthen dam broke, 125 people died within a period of two hours. Again survivors told of seeing family, friends, and neighbors being swept away by the raging waters. When Mr. Deitz wrote the flood books, he interviewed on tape the people who had experienced these events first hand, then wrote down the stories as they were told to him. Recent acts of terror and heroism will make these stories more poignant to readers. The Buffalo Creek book contains nearly 295 pictures depicting that horrible event. This tragic flood has been featured many times on the History Channel. Another program about the flood will soon be seen in an ABC news special with Dianne Sawyer.

Mr. Deitz has published two children's books. "The Little Spooner Who Wouldn't Spoon" was written to answer a question by a fourth grade girl who couldn't understand how so many siblings were able to share the same bedroom and especially the same bed back in the "olden days". You may want to find out just what "spooning" is. "Haunting in the Graveyard" was written by a budding author and great grandson of Mr. Deitz, Luke Deitz, when he was five years old. One of Luke's favorite holidays was Halloween and he enjoyed letting his imagination run wild. He also did the artwork in the book.

"Moms" was written in memory of Mr. Deitz' deceased wife, Madeline Deitz, who passed away in 1996. It is a compilation of remembrances written by those who knew and loved her. Although it is a very personal book, many who have read it have decided to keep the memories of their loved ones alive by doing something similar.

Two additional books written by Deitz were original novels. "The Search for Emily" is a historical novel of the Civil War. This is a story of young love, being separated by a long and cruel war, the struggle for survival, and somehow being united again. Deitz tried to keep the background, time, and place historically accurate. "A Promise Kept" is a book of short stories again dealing with the Civil War. This is a tragic love story based on a true story. This novel has also been transformed into a play and was performed at the Historical

Fayetteville Theater and at Tamarack. He also has a cassette tape of a short story called "Molly". This is the story of a young white girl who was captured by Indians. She was able to escape by convincing the Indians that she had strange powers because of her light, blonde hair. Other tapes Deitz has produced are the Greenbrier Ghost and the Turnpike Ghost Stories.

The "Bill Derenge Story" is a true story about a man who saved the lives of 42 men caught in a mine explosion by making them block themselves off from the "Black Damp" or carbon monoxide for five days until they could be rescued. He was also aided in his efforts by a young, Italian immigrant who spoke poor English, but helped them have hope by his cheerful disposition and his angel.

In spite of the fact that Mr. Deitz was a "late starter" in the field of writing, he has received much acclaim. He has received two awards from Tamarack, recognizing him for his efforts as a West Virginia author. Governor Cecil Underwood also bestowed upon Deitz the highest award that can be given to a citizen of the state - The Governor's Distinguished West Virginian Award. Of course, Deitz's favorite thing is to just sit and talk to folks he meets around the country.

Deitz says, "The big thing about writing is if you have a good story, then it is going to work out." Be assured that like his other books, "Greenbrier Ghost #3" is full of the kind of good stories that will make you want to share it with all in your family, young and old.

Bev Davis

TABLE OF CONTENTS

Acknowledgements iii

Foreword iv

The Dream .... by Adam Henson 1

The Little Boy .... by Ginger Phillips 2

Aunt Rachel's House .... by Sandy Schoolcraft 3

The Apartment .... by Allison Ledbetter 6

Donna Bailes Spends a Night at the General Lewis Inn
                                          by Dennis Deitz 8

The Ghosts of Droop Mountain .... by Terry Lowry 9

Droop Mountain .... by Jeremiah Manahan 15

A Presence .... by Rick Elkins 16

Visitor in the Hallway .... by Betty Shreve 17

A Last Goodbye .... by Carlene Mowery 19

The Little Girl from the Cemetery ..... by Johnny Faye Lane 21

Ghost Premonition .... by Arnout Hyde 23

Only in the Picture .... by Jackie Skaggs 24

On the Twelve Hour Shift .... by Carrie Kinsie 25

TABLE OF CONTENTS — *Continued*

The Watson's .... by Dee Morton 27

As Close as You Can Get .... by Franklin Austin 29

Charlie .... by Robin Williamson 30

The Man in the Brown Suit .... by Ginger Phillips 32

Strange Happenings .... by Linda Moore 34

Mommy's Stories .... by Glenna Hager 42

Amanda's Angel .... by Amanda Winnell 46

The Estep Family Guardian .... by Chris Estep 48

Ghostly Guest, or How I Met My Father In Law
  .... by Karla Arveson 51

Return For a Drink .... by Susan Pettit 53

The Bell Witch .... by Dennis Deitz 54

St. Francis Ghost .... by Sheila Scott 56

The Family Curse .... by Candice Lynch 57

The Devil's Fire .... by Candice Lynch 58

Comforting Spirits in the Cumberland Plateau
  .... by Suzette Roberts 59

Why Me Lord? .... by Diana Linn Miller 64

Remembering the Braxton County Monster
  .... by Dennis Deitz 70

TABLE OF CONTENTS — *Continued*

Braxton Monster .... Interview with Fred May ... 71

Kathleen May Horner .... by Bessie Hawkins 73

Kathleen May Horner and the Braxton County Monster 78

Invasion of the Green Monsters .... by James Gay Jones 81

Something Green and Orange .... by Dexter Pritt 84

The Sighting .... by Ruth E. Lears 85

True Ghost and Other Odd Stories ... by Michelle Henson 87

Ghostbusting .... by Juanita Teeters 90

And There I Was at Twenty Thousand Feet
.... by Robert Evans 92

Grandma's House .... by Joel Neace 95

Freddie .... by Sandy Colegrove 96

Samson .... by Don Vance 101

Grandmother's Perceptions .... by Margie Pullen 102

Grandmother's Role .... By Mike King 104

The Bus .... By Charlotte Vance 106

The Dream
By Adam Henson

A few years ago, there was an old couple living in St. Albans who loved to fish. They had a boat and many fishing accessories. They loved to fish up and down the Kanawha River all year long.

One hot day they were out on their boat. There were many other boaters and jet skiers out at the time. Without warning, a jet skier, distracted by the noise from a nearby train, suddenly crashed into them and split the boat in half. The man survived, but the woman didn't. Within months of the tragic accident, the old man had lost all interest in fishing and moped around like he didn't want to live. He sold all of his fishing gear and was about to give up all hope. Shortly thereafter, the old man had a very disturbing dream. His wife came to him and told him to get all of his fishing gear back and go to a certain spot under the Southside Bridge in Charleston. He tried to ignore the dream and went on moping around as usual.

A week later he had the same exact dream, but this time she even gave him a time to be at that certain spot under the bridge. This time the old man decided to listen to his wife and bought a new rod, reel, boat, and everything he needed to fish on the river. He went out the next day and fished under the bridge. He couldn't understand why she was sending him to that spot. When he arrived, he looked up to see a man on the bridge with his head in his hands like he was crying. He watched as the young man suddenly climbed over the railing and jumped. The old man sped over to the young man as he struggled against the current. He pulled him into the boat just in the nick of time and took him to shore. By that time, an ambulance was waiting.

Several days later, while visiting the young man in the hospital, the old man told him what had happened to his wife and about the dreams. The young man also told the old man about his problems and why he had jumped. Over the next several years, the old man helped the young man get his life back together, and the old man had someone to care about. This way the old man knew that his wife was still with him - maybe not in person, but in heart and soul.

THE LITTLE BOY
By Ginger Phillips

I am a flight attendant for a major airline. One of our various duties is lifting tickets or, in other words, taking a passengers electronic ticket or flight coupon prior to boarding the aircraft.

A few months ago I was in Houston, Texas, doing just that. There was a line of about fifteen people waiting to board the aircraft. In my peripheral view, I noticed a little boy dancing around his father's leg. The dad was about the fifth or sixth person standing in line waiting for me to pull his ticket. When I lift tickets, I pay attention to several things on the ticket; the date, the correct flight number, and the correct flight segment. Needless to say, my attention is more on what I am doing than the people standing in line. But, I noticed this little boy because he seemed so excited as he was dancing around and between his dad's legs. The father was not paying any attention to the young boy because he was talking to a fellow traveler standing in line in front of him. As the man reached the podium for me to take his ticket, he only handed me one ticket for himself. I asked him if he had a ticket for his son, and he said he was by himself. I looked behind the man and around the boarding area for the little boy but he was not there. He was not anywhere in the boarding area. I finished loading the plane and I went on the plane and told my fellow-flying partner what just happened. She said, "Wow, that sends chills through my body!"

AUNT RACHEL'S HOUSE

By Sandy Schoolcraft

When I was five years old, my family went to visit relatives. My aunt and uncle had a big house with 5 acres outside of Columbus, OH.

It was dark by the time that we arrived. We went into the house. Rachel, my aunt, told us to come into the living room. For some reason, I was looking at my dad when we stepped into the living room. All of a sudden my dad's eyes got really big and he dropped the suitcases. I tugged on his sleeve and told him that I wanted to go home. My Aunt Rachel laughed and said, "Oh, you see my ghost".

There in the hallway was a silhouette of a man. It had a light behind the silhouette. This figure would go down one side of the wall and then to the other side. I wanted to go home right then! But dad said that we had to stay. Then, to make matters worse, they put me upstairs in the room across from them located in the attic. As I went to sleep, I had the sensation that someone was breathing on my neck. I screamed and screamed. Finally, mom and dad decided that in order for them to get any rest, I would be allowed to sleep with them (where the ghost couldn't get me).

The ghost would always breathe on you in the attic. I got kind of used to it during the day, but I made sure that I was never alone up there. One evening, we went to the store. When we returned, my aunt locked the door to her car and we carried the groceries into the house. I went into the bathroom to put the toilet paper underneath the sink. The sink door was already open and inside there was a plastic, faded rose, the kind you see in the cemetery, with a long black hair on it. I asked my aunt why she kept that old flower with the hair on it. She replied that she did not know where the rose had come from. I showed her where I found it. Nobody had a clue as to how the flower had gotten there. Later, as we were getting ready for bed, Uncle Charles came through the front door screaming at everyone. We were confused and asked, "What's going on?" Uncle Charles was angry with Aunt Rachel because he had supposed that Aunt Rachel forgot to lock the doors to the car and had assumed that something had happened to everyone because the car doors and trunk were all wide open!

Many strange things happened in that house. On one occasion, my Aunt Helen and Uncle Adam came to visit the house with their 8 month old baby named Ernie. Ernie had asthma and wheezed loudly when asleep. Adam and Helen placed him in the crib in the attic and went to bed. Aunt Rachel heard a wheezing sound outside their bedroom door, which was downstairs. She opened the door and there lay Ernie, fast asleep. She carried him upstairs and woke Aunt Helen and Uncle Adam. No one knew how Ernie had gotten downstairs. They put him in the crib and went back to sleep. Awhile later, Rachel was awakened again by a wheezing sound. Sure enough, when she opened the door, there was the baby. The baby did not know how to crawl yet. Finally, everyone slept downstairs in the living room.

One time my cousins and I (there were 5 of us children) were all upstairs. We were all laughing and talking when suddenly there was a loud bang. It sounded like a Chinese gong. We did not know where the noise came from so we ran downstairs. Sometimes that loud gong would scare us outside the house. It felt a lot safer outside than inside with the ghost!

Uncle Charles and Aunt Rachel had a cornfield on their property. My cousins and I decided that it would be a good idea to see where the cornfield ended. So, my cousin Cheryl and I went in the cornfield. Before we were ready to go in, we could hear birds chirping loudly, lawn mowers, traffic, etc., but just a little way in, there was silence. We continued to walk on, my cousin Cheryl was in front and I was behind her. I noticed the crunching footsteps behind me. I thought that one of the other cousins had decided to follow us. There was nothing behind us, so we ran! The crunching got louder but no one was there. We became really scared and changed directions and ran toward the house. No one had been near the cornfield except for us.

When Rachel had purchased the house, the owners were jumping up and down in excitement, which was peculiar to Aunt Rachel. Since that time, Aunt Rachel has sold the house and moved. The last I heard, no one was living there.

THE APARTMENT
By Allison Ledbetter

I attended college at Montseriat College of Art, located on the North Shore of Boston in a small, historical town called Beverly. The age and folklore of Eastern Massachusetts amazed me. Before I moved there, I had lived in commercialized, new Virginia Beach. Much was rumored about several of the dorm apartments - ghost stories, strange sounds - I didn't really believe in most of it, figuring the stories were created and believed mainly due to the closeness of Salem, MA, and the stories and history behind the Salem Witch Trials.

Despite my unwillingness to believe, certain occurrences eventually changed my mind. The apartment I had lived in during my freshman year was a relatively new building, but it gave a sense of old, troubled past. After a bit of research, I discovered that the plot of land my building was erected on was originally the home of one of the Puritan settlers.

After a few weeks of living there, there were times I felt uneasy being home alone. I heard voices in the walls, saw things out of the corner of my eye; but, I still believed that nothing was amiss. I chalked it up to an overactive imagination. One night, sometime in early October, none of my three roommates or I could sleep. We all felt uneasy, as if something were wrong.

We brewed some coffee and gathered in our living room for sleepy discussions. My roommate Emily, finally admitted to seeing and hearing things. By the looks on everyone's faces, she and I weren't the only ones. We decided not to talk about it again, but none of us wanted to sleep alone. We pulled blankets into the living room and crashed on the floor for the rest of the night.

Time passed, and still nothing was said about our strange apartment . . .until Columbus Day weekend.

Two of my roommates, Emily and Emma, went home for the long weekend. Meghan and I stayed, and a friend of Meghan's was staying with us. The two of them had gone out for dinner, while I went next door to visit for a while. We all returned to the apartment at around the same time.

After unlocking the door, I noticed a strange smell. It was like oranges, but very strong. I noticed that the window was closed, although I was sure I'd left it open a crack. While I rushed across the room to open the window and air the room out, Meghan discovered where the smell was coming from. A solvent we used to clean our paintbrushes, Citre-Solv, had been poured down her desk, on the carpet and throughout the room on the furniture. The odd part is that our apartment was locked, and the jars of Citre-Solv we kept on the table were unmoved. I walked across the living room to the kitchen, bewildered - and realized that all 4 burners of our gas stove were on "high". Flames were leaping from each burner's center.

That's when I realized the seriousness of the situation. Had we not returned when we did, our building would have exploded! The dangerous fumes from the solvent, the closed window, and the open flame from the stovetop could have made a huge chemical fire had the situation been left long enough. We turned off the stove, aired out the apartment and sat down to review our options.

There was no sign of a break-in. The door was locked and our window was three stories off the ground. No one had a key, other than the roommates. Emma was in New York, Emily was in Chicago, and there was only the two of us left.

DONNA BAILES SPENDS A NIGHT AT THE GENERAL LEWIS INN
By Dennis Deitz

Donna Bailes lives in Florida and while taking a vacation to West Virginia in October 1999 met a long time friend, Dr. Charles Lake.

Dr. Lake graciously invited her on a trip to Lewisburg for a special tour of historic homes in the area. Lewisburg is a beautiful town and takes pride in preserving its history. Many old, beautiful and perhaps haunted homes were open for public viewing.

Dr. Lake called the General Lewis Inn for reservations and booked the last two rooms available - 119 for himself and 121 for Donna Bailes. After the tour and a late dinner they made arrangements for breakfast with friends.

Mrs. Bailes went to her room, locked her door, went to bed and to sleep. Sometime later something woke her. She heard light steps crossing the room. She kept her eyes closed, too scared to open them. Then she felt the other side of her double bed sink down as though a fairly light person had laid down on the bed. She had the impression it was a woman. She still kept her eyes closed - maybe believing that if she didn't see a ghost the ghost wouldn't see her. She then heard someone saying softly "Bill-Bill". Eyes still closed she got up enough nerve to fling an arm across the bed. It was empty! It was a long, long night trying to sleep with a ghost in the bed.

The next morning they had breakfast with friends from Bluefield, Dr. and Mrs. Kiser. When she shared her story with them, they didn't laugh at all but shared a similar experience that had happened that night in their room.

Mrs. Bailes then asked the night clerk about her room and the clerk said that she did double duty cleaning rooms. Lights in room 121 would flick on and off without anyone being around.

For years, I had heard of strange occurrences at the General Lewis Inn but had never found anyone who had actually been involved and would share their story. Thank you, Donna Bailes!

THE GHOSTS OF DROOP MOUNTAIN
By Terry Lowry

While it is fairly common for ghost stories to arise out of Civil War sites, Droop Mountain probably ranks near, or even at the top, of such areas to spawn wild-eyed stories about ghosts, apparitions headless soldiers, illusions, and the like. Due primarily to its somewhat isolated, rural location, Droop Mountain battlefield has been the scene of many unexplained happenings since the Civil War battle that took place there in 1863. This is not unusual, considering fog "often rolls over the mountain in waves, there one minute, gone the next," creating an eerie atmosphere conducive to tales of ghosts and the supernatural. As park superintendent Mike Smith so aptly stated, "It's the general feeling of everybody that ghosts of soldiers are nearby. Some people have told about hearing supernatural horse hooves, some so real that they thought they were going to be run over. Other people have said that they have been going through the park at night and have been stopped in the road by a Union soldier who won't let them go until dawn."

The earliest known episode of a supernatural occurrence at Droop Mountain took place in 1865 when Betty and Nancy Snedegar, residents of the west side of Droop and daughters of James C. and Rebecca Kellison Snedegar, walked to the east side of the mountain to pick berries. On their return trip, they located two guns apparently lost during the battle two years earlier. As the two girls "started to carry off the guns, rocks were thrown at them but they saw no person. They went on home. As they went to milk, more rocks and clubs were thrown at them. At the house rocks came down the chimney and knocked the lids off the pots. Rocks came through the log walls, but left no holes. There were sheepskin rugs on the floor which started rarin' up . . ." Another account claims the sheepskin rug would stand erect and bawl. The Snedegar sister then ". . . gathered all the rocks and threw them in a sinkhole several [hundred?] feet deep. The rocks all came flyin' back out." One version of the story claimed "dog irons would come out of the fireplace and race around the room." Reportedly, an uncle came to visit and two rocks hit him in the arm and head. After this, he quickly departed. Finally, the guns were returned to their original location and all the problems ceased.

The next known account of a supernatural event took place in 1914 when F. W. Albert spotted a regiment of soldiers on the battlefield, marching two by two, each carrying a gun on his shoulder.

Edgar Walton, an elder resident of Droop Mountain who once lived in the old Sunrise schoolhouse about a quarter of a mile from the park entrance, recalled that in 1920 he and a friend were walking together when they stopped to build a fire and noticed an unusual apparition. Mr. Walton stated, "I never did believe in ghosts and still don't, but we saw something. It was in the form of a man but without a head, and it was drifting along." In another conversation Walton related the same story in more detail and said the incident took place in 1927. He remembered, "I was walking near Spring Creek Mountain with a friend. I wanted to go over the mountain, but he wouldn't come that way. We sat down near an old root pile to rest and broke up a bunch of dry roots to build a fire." Walton continued, "I heard something that sounded like somebody dragging a hand through the leaves. I turned around and there was this soldier standing as close to me as this . . .My friend says, 'Let's get out of here.' The ghost walked to the middle of the gate and it disappeared. It might have had clothes on, but there was no head to it. And it didn't walk. It just drifted along."

Such stories of headless soldiers at Droop Mountain obviously are based upon the actual incident during the battle in which 2nd Lt. Joseph W. Daniels, Battery B, 1st West Virginia Light Artillery, had his head shot off by a Confederate shell. Although a Yankee, most storytellers prefer Confederates as ghosts, therefore, through endless folklore, Daniels has apparently become a rebel.

A great example of the headless soldier story was told by Anna Atkins, who grew up on Droop Mountain. She related that during the battle a mounted soldier encountered an enemy foot soldier about where Gerald Brown would reside in 1981. The trooper grabbed an infantryman by the hair and sliced off his head with his sword. Anna said, "He is supposed to have thrown the head in a pond nearby but no one ever found the head. The body was buried on the side of the road on G. Brown's front property." As a result of this incident, in the years following, "when horses passed there at night, the ghost - a headless man - stood by the horses and held them by the bridle bit until daylight; then they could proceed. One night a driver with a double team was stopped. He urged the team on. Still they stood. Finally he saw the ghost holding the bridle bits of the lead team. Kindly he asked it to release the horses. In desperation he grabbed his blacksnake whip, walked out the wagon tongue, sprang to the back of a horse and came down on the headless ghost several times. The horses bolted and ran, the driver clung to a mane. His buddies, who were part of a wagon team, stopped the wagon down the road. That was the last time the ghost held horses back."

Henry J. Johnson, one of 220 enrollees at CCC Camp Price on Droop Mountain in 1935, recalled that during his tenure, "Tales were told of the sound of marching feet on moonless nights around the perimeter of the camp." Johnson's co-workers, visiting girlfriends in the area, "would scurry through the darkened woods and bring tales of ghostly 'Who goes there?' challenges. The screaming bobcats at the camp dump and the cries of the large owls that emanated from the darkened forest served to add to the eerie aura surrounding a luckless night time traveler. Only the bravest of CCC workers ventured alone at night into an area alive with memories of those who had fallen and died there."

In 1941 Johnnie Keen had been driving a heavy-duty two ton lumber truck since 3:30 the morning before. He encountered a ghostly apparition "just below the long straight stretch as you reach the front of Droop on [the] south side in the first curve beyond [the] home known at that time as the Brown's residence." The confrontation took place at about 2:30 A.M. when Keen arrived at the curve and spotted in his headlight beam "about 8 or 12 people riding horses and they were riding fairground or showhorse style." He slammed on his brakes, got out of the vehicle to talk, but the group quickly turned to the left and disappeared. Keen said they, "were wearing men's khaki-colored pants, blue jackets . . .[trousers] similar to what chauffeurs would wear . . . an army officer. The front horse on the left of the group that approached me was white. Others were bay or darker colored and each was carrying saddle bags as though they were cavalry."

Napoleon Holbrook, who served as park superintendent from 1946-49, recalled a number of episodes that affected him and his family while residing at the park. One morning at 3:00 A.M. he heard a screaming sound that came from the direction of the cranberry bog in the park. Holbrook reflected, "It could have been an animal, but it was real enough sounding that I got up and went to look, but I didn't find anything."

Holbrook experienced a number of incidents, such as the day his son was playing in the road in front of the park office and heard a horse riding toward him. "The noise came so close it scared him and he ran inside." At another time Holbrook's six year old daughter Carole was playing in the pine trees in front of the park residence when she spotted a man in a knee-length Confederate coat lying against a tree as if asleep. Carole stated, "It was very real to me."

Also during Holbrook's residency at the park, Mrs. Holbrook once heard footsteps on the back porch of the park residence. Nap emphasized, "She swears to this day that the footsteps went to a cellar near the back porch, and that the lock jiggled." And in another episode; one Sunday afternoon, as the Holbrook family was in the park residence, Carole remembered, "We clearly and distinctly heard a shout, 'Halt!' outside . . .it sounded like it came from the front porch. But when we looked there wasn't anybody around."

Two park superintendents, Clyde Crowley, who served from 1950-52, and E. Morris Harsh, from 1952-54, both reported no ghostly experiences during their tenures. However, William Davis, park superintendent from 1959-68, told of the day he was working in the park with caretaker Floyd Clutter when the two heard a scream of distress. Clutter said, "We searched the woods and didn't find anyone. . . Bill had planned to go somewhere, but he stayed at the park because he was certain someone was in trouble." Davis added, "During the time we were at Droop we heard noises we simply considered house noises . . .but I couldn't explain the scream, and it never was explained. It's possible someone could have been on one of the hiking trails, but we searched the area and there didn't appear to have been anyone around."

In 1970 Mrs. John Clutter of Renick, mother of Floyd Clutter, park caretaker from 1968-84, said that while at the park she saw a man standing beside the soldiers' graves in the rear of the park residence. She said, "He stepped behind a tree and didn't reappear . . .I went to look and there wasn't anybody there."

Clarence Murray, a Department of Highways engineer who resided near the park, went squirrel hunting in October of 1972 and heard a sound like horses pulling a wagon, accompanied by jingling sounds. Murray reported, "I have no reason to lie about it . . .I did hear it and it did sound like hoofbeats. It was close, like it was going to run over me." Despite the sound Murray said he saw nothing.

In 1975 Mrs. Jean Murphy (a Clutter relative) of Akron, Ohio, was spending the night at the park when she awoke feeling a presence in the room. Mrs. Murphy told an interviewer, "It wasn't anything I saw . . .it was more like a presence, an evil presence. I kept trying to convince myself I wasn't awake, but I was. I prayed and prayed, and at the first glimmer of dawn, the presence left. I can't sleep in that room anymore."

Caretaker Floyd Clutter made it clear that neither he nor his wife believed in ghosts, but said that on July 16, 1977, at about 10 P.M., the Clutters and several relatives had returned from church and were in the park residence kitchen eating. Floyd said, "All of us clearly heard somebody coming up on the porch, we heard the door open and we heard sounds like youngsters talking . . .yet when I went into the living room there wasn't anybody there, and the door was locked." Mrs. Clutter experienced another odd scene during a night of August 1977 as she sat at home alone watching television. She heard a knocking sound on the outside wall near the television and looked out the window to see a hat like the one Mr. Clutter wore floating past the window. She said, "It just floated out into the darkness . . .the porch light was on and I couldn't have imagined it."

The Clutters also mentioned that two summers prior to 1977 they heard a knock at the front door. "It was as natural as you'd want any knock to be," Floyd recalled, "but when I went to the door, there wasn't anybody there." This may be the same event that took place at about 3:30 P.M. on a spring day when Mrs. Clutter heard a loud knock on the front door. "It was like someone was rattling the door to get my attention . . .Floyd had gone to town, and I thought he had come back and didn't have his key. But when I went to the door, there was nobody there." Mrs. Clutter claimed the same occurrence transpired three times that afternoon, but each time there was nothing to be found.

The Clutters have also told of similar encounters, including the sound of car doors slamming shut but no cars being located, and have concluded that at least the ghosts are polite since, "The noises almost always happen in the daytime . . . We rarely hear anything at night," and the ghosts only come around every two or three months.

The headless ghost-soldier story arose again in 1977 when Mrs. Clenston Delaney, daughter of Edgar Walton, along with her husband and sister, spotted a headless, ghost-like figure on the same spot as her father in 1920 [27?]. She said it took place one evening while cutting wood near the battlefield, when they "saw an apparition that left them frightened and shaking." The headless ghost, clad in a gray uniform, floated past her making a moaning sound. Mrs. Delaney declared, "It was very odd. I can't explain it. But all three of us saw it."

As recent as 1990, Tom Nelson of Parkersburg, West Virginia, who served as a Civil War living history re-enactor as a Private in Co. F (Night Hawk Rangers), 17th Virginia Cavalry, claimed he saw a dapple gray horse with a grayish blurred image atop it. "There is no doubt in my mind I saw a gray horse that night on Droop Mountain," Nelson relayed, but "As to whether it was any form of a ghost I cannot say."

Present park superintendent Mike Smith does not believe in ghosts, and said, he has yet to see one at Droop, but he also refuses to discount the possibilities. Smith believes the tales made good fodder for tourists and says, "I don't know for sure. I am somewhat skeptical, but I hate to say those tales are not true." Whether or not Smith is correct, it is certain Droop Mountain battlefield will continue to spawn weird tales of ghosts, headless soldiers, apparitions, and things that go bump in the night.

From the Book *The Last Sleep: The Battle of Droop Mountain* by Terry Lowry

DROOP MOUNTAIN
By Jeremiah Manahan

My name is Jeremiah Manahan. I've lived here in the Greenbrier/Pocahontas County region for 16 years now. After my step daddy died in 1988, we heard strange sounds that couldn't be explained. My mother, truly believes that it was him coming back to say his last respects and to see the land for the last time.

I've heard this noise on several occasions. I haven't heard it now for several years, and it was nothing I had heard before. Not animal, not human. I'd be standing on one end of the mountain on top of the ridge and I could hear it to the right, to left, behind, and in front of me for a few seconds.

I've tried to look for it, tried to find tracks. I've listened to different sounds on tape trying to get a clue as to what it might be and I've not been able to find it yet.

A PRESENCE
By Rick Elkins

My name is Rick Elkins, and I'm from Barboursville, West Virginia. This event took place ten to fifteen years ago around Barboursville.

I worked for a gentleman who had his own warehouse on his property. Several of his family said that they had seen strange things happen. My experience started when we were timbering his property and had cut a tree down. I was trying to get the tree out of the woods before it got dark. I wanted to hook a chain to it and attach it to the tractor. I felt a presence around me, and heard several noises. I got the chain around the tree but it was too big for me to reach around with both arms. As I stuck one arm over the top of the tree to get to the end of the chain, the chain was already there, halfway up the side of the tree where I couldn't reach. It was as if somebody had picked it up and handed it to me.

VISITOR IN THE HALLWAY
By Betty Shreve

My name is Betty Shreve. I am at Droop Mountain Battleground. We have been doing this event for about 10 years now. We have raised our children here. We have heard all of these stories about the ghost. We just kind of took it like fun stuff. We told the kids, "Yeah, go look in the woods for the ghost." Everybody just had fun with it.

We do reenacting, but at night I stay in a motor home, not in a tent. The motor home is very secure. It is locked up; everything is fine. We went to bed at 11:30pm. We were super-tired after driving and getting here. I couldn't fall asleep. Everytime I would try to go to sleep, I would hear a noise and couldn't figure out what it was. I was finally just about to fall asleep when I heard another noise. I opened my eyes and there was a figure standing right in the doorway. Not exactly the doorway, but a hallway in the motor home, if you can see, from the bedroom to the front section. I called out to my husband thinking it was him. I looked beside me and saw that he was in bed beside me sleeping. I called out two more times, and by the third time, I was scared because I had realized it was not my husband, and he wasn't responding because he was asleep - he was out. When I hollered out the third time louder to him and turned, it was gone. This is the first time, I thought, I have been haunted at

Droop. It literally scared me to death. It was the first time in my fifty years I had been afraid of the dark.

I realized that the figure was a man but I do not want to add any detail that was not there. It would be very easy to decorate the story. I also know that it was not a prowler because if the door had opened, I would have heard it. We have four dogs staying with us in the motor home. If anything like that goes by the motor home, or in it, they bark and holler and wake us up. It was very, very quiet outside, and all of a sudden, there was this person - in a suit. I couldn't see the front part of the suit, but I could tell that it was a jacket and some pants. He was very calm, just standing there looking at us. And then he was gone.

For once, I am a believer in the Droop Mountain ghost stories. I do not think that it is here to hurt people, or to scare people. I had a feeling it was a soldier. I couldn't tell if it was blue or gray. He just looked at me like something was out of place - like are you supposed to be here or am I supposed to be here? The whole feeling was really strange. I am a believer now. Not having anything on our mind, and then to see that. They're here this weekend - the soldiers. We're just the re-enactors. I have a greater respect for the battle - the men who fought and died here. I get teary-eyed now, because I actually believe that there is something here now.

A LAST GOODBYE
By Carlene Mowery

When I was growing up, I was never around my father's side of the family much. They were more distant, private people when compared to my mother's side of the family. I was a sophomore in high school before I ever met my great uncle, Berry.

I went with my parents to visit him in the hospital, which was located across from the high school. He was in an oxygen tent and had a great deal of difficulty breathing. When my parents introduced me to him, he looked at me with a smile and slowly slipped his hand under the oxygen tent and lovingly squeezed my hand.

I felt a warmth from that touch that seemed to bond us together from that moment on. I studied his face carefully, and beyond the pale, wrinkled, grey haired form before me, I saw a lonely, humble man who yearned for the slightest word of kindness from those gathered in the room. I couldn't help but wonder what I had missed from not having known him during the years I was growing up.

After leaving his room, the family all gathered outside to discuss his condition. It seemed there was no improvement at all. Every day he grew weaker.

I caught myself looking back down the long, dark corridor to his room and thinking how lonely he must feel having to be away from his family, realizing, too, that he was near death. I felt a sadness I had never known before.

The next day at school, I couldn't keep from thinking about him being alone there in that hospital bed, and of the loving way he touched my hand and the gleam in his eyes from the slightest friendly gesture.

When my lunch period came, I hurried to the hospital to visit with him. He looked surprised to see me when I walked into the room. He couldn't speak, but I saw a tear fall from his eye and slip down his cheek, and I knew that my visit meant much to him.

I had very little time to spend, since I had to hurry back to school and I wanted the time we had together to be quality time. Conversation was hard for me since I had just met him and I didn't know what to talk about because we had no memories to share that we could reflect back on, and I didn't think he'd be interested in the things we talked about in school. All I knew is that I wanted to be of comfort to him and just be there to dispel the loneliness I knew he was feeling. I opened my purse and took out my New Testament and I sat by his bedside and read to him. When it was time to go, I stood and looked through the veil of the oxygen tent that surrounded him and with a slight nod of his head, he said goodbye. Every day for the next 2 weeks, I sat by his bedside and read to him and he listened intently.

One night I woke from a sound sleep and sat upright in my bed. I had never done that before, and I thought it must be time to get up and get ready for school but when I looked at the clock, I saw it was only 3:30 in the morning. Suddenly, Uncle Berry came to my mind and I wondered if he was okay. I couldn't go back to sleep for thinking of him, so I got out of bed and knelt down and said a prayer for him. I then went back to sleep.

Mom woke me at the usual time, and as my brothers and sisters and I gathered around the breakfast table she said, 'Your Uncle Berry died last night about 3:30.

I was heartbroken. Even though the time we had spent together was brief, I felt it had been quality time, and I felt a peace within myself. I thought back to the early morning hour when I woke thinking of him, and realized that he had come to say goodbye to me.

THE LITTLE GIRL FROM THE CEMETERY

By Johnny Faye Lane

My name is Johnny Faye Lane. I was named after my dad, Johnny. My mother's name is Marritta. We live in Lucasville, Ohio and just behind our house is the Lucasville prison. Our house sits where the old, one room schoolhouse once sat. I remember starting kindergarten the year we moved in.

About 4 years after we moved into the house, my sister, Sharon, who was about 19 at the time, was home alone that evening. She was in the living room flipping the channels on the TV, trying to find something to watch. She glanced over to the dining room for a second, and she saw a little girl standing there. She was about 5 or 6 years old with long brown hair almost to her waist. Sharon blinked her eyes and looked again and the little girl disappeared. She turned back around and started flipping the channels again and all of a sudden she heard the pots and pans being thrown to the floor. She ran into the dining room and saw several pots and pans in the floor but they were all stacked together instead of being scattered. She picked up the pots and pans and put them on the counter. She got so scared she ran and got 2 Bibles and put them under the pillow in dad's room and then she locked the door and went to bed. The next morning when she woke up, the door was unlocked but nothing was out of place.

A little while after that, my grandmother, Nan, brought a Ouija board to the house. Mom and I were sitting at the dining room table playing it. When I went to bed that night, it was about 2 or 3 in the morning. I woke up about 5 a.m. and I started to turn over in the bed when I saw a little girl standing near the foot of my bed. The light from the dining room was shining in the room and I could see her clearly. She was about 5 or 6 years old and had long straight brown hair almost to her waist. She was looking into the dining room. She had on a brown dress with short sleeves just like a dress I had. I started to sit up in the bed to see if I could see her face, but she disappeared. I got so scared I ran and got in bed with my mom and I slept there for weeks because I was afraid to go back into my room.

Mom finally told me I had to sleep in my room, I couldn't stay in there with her anymore. I started sleeping on the couch instead, but I did finally go back to sleeping in my room. After Sharon and I both saw the little girl, mom got out the Ouija board and we all sat around the table and asked it questions about the little girl and it said her name was Jamie and she had died from the fever and she was buried in the cemetery by our house.

There's an old cemetery beside our house and on one of the tombstones is the last name "Marsh". They're so old we can't make out the rest of the writing. We haven't seen the little girl anymore since.

Mom finally burned the Ouija board in our grill that dad made for us.

GHOST PREMONITION
by Arnout Hyde

It was about 5:30 am on a misty morning with lots of fog. I was photographing Burnside Bridge at the Antietam Battlefield when 4 or 5 broken voices issuing rapid commands, seemed to seep out of the ground for about 30 seconds. I could only make out a few words - like- Hurry, Backup, Move. There was no one physically there.

ONLY IN THE PICTURE
By Jackie Skaggs

My name is Jackie Skaggs. A girlfriend and I were driving through a place called Dunn's Gap, VA. I have been through there numerous times. It is just a little dirt road with a beautiful little gorge. For some reason, something told me to stop the car. I got out and was looking around. My girlfriend said, "Why don't you take a picture of the gorge for me." I took the picture for her. When I got out of the car, I got this real eerie, nasty feeling. Not a good feeling, it was like someone wanted to hurt me.

I worked at a photo shop at the time. I developed the film and printed the pictures. When I looked at one of the pictures, there was a man with a hatchet in his hand coming up over the hill, coming at me. He was coming right at me. He was not ten feet from where I was standing. I couldn't make it out while taking the picture, but the camera picked it up. I thought no wonder I had that funny feeling. It was in the picture, but did not show up on the negative. The man had on a gray jacket, gray pants, and a slouch hat and had a hatchet in his hands. It was like he was protecting his territory. He was coming after me. He was going to kill me.

This man was in six or eight of the pictures; however, he did not show up in the negatives. He was in a different pose in each shot. It was like he was actually in motion. The expression on his face was like he was so angry - like you don't belong here. You could see the detail of the eyes, the whole nine yards.

ON THE TWELVE HOUR SHIFT
By Carrie Kinsie

My name is Carrie Kinsie. I live in Fairmont, WV. I am a registered nurse. This incident happened when I was a 12 hour nurse at United Hospital in Clarksburg. There was a lady who came in who was terminally ill. She was 79 years old. She lasted for about a week. The other staff members and I didn't really know how she made it, but her last words were that she did not want to die until her 80th birthday, which was in a week. We took care of her for a week. We didn't know how she could live without eating or drinking. She became very cyanotic around the ears, almost purple black from her body systems deteriorating.

On her eightieth birthday, I came in. I was on 12 hour - 7 p.m. to 7 a.m. About the middle of the shift, she died. Her last words were that she wanted to die on her eightieth birthday because she wanted to celebrate with Jesus, so that wish came true for her.

This story took place in the fall. It took us about an hour and a half to get her body ready for the morgue. We cleaned her up and got her prepared. I would say about a half hour later (her room had already been cleaned) that the television set came on. We went in and turned it off and shut the doors. Probably about fifteen or twenty minutes later, the call button came on. There was nobody in this room - at all. This went on all night for the twelve hour shift. The call bell would come on and we would turn it off. We had maintenance come up and look at it, but they said there was nothing wrong. The TV or the lights would come on. The channels on the TV would turn. You had to use the call bell to change the channels. To get the call bell on you would have to use the clicker. You have to hold it. It's a hand held set. The lights, you would actually have to pull a string attached at the head of the bed or turn a switch on.

I was with an old-fashioned LPN and she absolutely believes that it was that lady's spirit. We ended up closing the room. We told the supervisor and closed the room for that twelve hour shift because all night long we were going in there to turn the lights off or the TV or the call bell.

I know that this lady didn't have any family. Before she died, we all surrounded her - all the nurses. There were about five of us, which is a good bit for the night shift. We held her hand and held hands and told her that it was ok to go to Jesus. I honestly believe that was her way of telling us that she was still there.

THE WATSON'S
By Dee Morton

My name is Dee Morton and I live in Jane Lew, West Virginia. We live in a one hundred year old farmhouse. There are ghosts there, but they are good ones. They have not been active in the last several years, so I guess they like what we have done adding on to the house and remodeling.

When the children were little (and we have four) we could hear old Mr. Watson (that's the person who built the house) walk through the upstairs, down the backstairs, out the kitchen door, and we assume he went to the chicken coop. There was no one upstairs. The children were too little to do this. There were no backstairs. The steps weren't there, but the sound was. It was as if someone was going down creaky stairs. You could hear the screen door. The gate was such that it could not have been a child.

There was another occasion, where I was cleaning feverishly, and the kitchen cabinet doors opened, and only the plastic glasses were thrust out. There had to have been a wife. It had to be a woman, because a man would not have thought to throw out just the stuff that wouldn't break. It was the early morning, and no one was up - not even my husband. There was a coke or soda container of some sort on the counter. It went back and forth and shook. I turned around and - I don't know why I did it - but I said, "Stop that!". It stopped.

One time I saw something out by the barn (what it was I could not say because it was hazy). The lady who was living next door to us at that point was a niece of the people who had built the house. She said that the lady did ride horses and there was a side saddle in there. Two years ago, I was taking pictures down by our creek which is in front of the house, and after I got the picture developed an image appeared in the water. We couldn't find out where the reflection was coming from. It was a young girl, dressed in an outfit that would have been of that era between 1888 and 1899. It was not a form fitting dress and it faded into the water so that we could not tell what the length was. It was apparently longer. It looked like she had a garland of flowers in her hair. She may have been in the woods playing and gathering flowers. None of these things were ever scary and we just always referred to it as Mr. and Mrs. Watson being about.

They seem to be most active when the kids were little and we were remodeling the old front of the house. We thought they must like what we were doing because nothing bad ever happened.

I haven't seen the Watson's since the photograph, which was entered into a photo contest. They seem to be content with us living in the house. Maybe they think we don't need to be watched.

AS CLOSE AS YOU CAN GET
By Franklin Austin

My name is Franklin Austin and I am from Beckley, WV. Many years ago my grandfather, Austin, told the tale about when one of his great aunts died a number of years after her husband. Her request was always to be buried as close as possible to her husband. Back then, the family dug the graves. My grandpa got some of his friends and family members and dug the grave. As they were digging, grandpa looked up and said, "Boys, I think we've dug deep enough." They buried his great aunt right on top of her husband. That's about as close as you can get.

CHARLIE
By Robin Williamson

My name is Robin Williamson and I am from Ona, WV. I can't say I believe in ghosts, but I know what I saw. What I saw in the Autumn of 1998 is something I will never forget. I lived in Martinsburg at the time, two doors down from the Apollo Theatre which used to be a speakeasy and now holds plays. My home at the time was a three story Victorian that overlooked the historical part of town, next to the round house. I lived on the second floor that had a beautiful bay window over the street. I used this room in the evenings to feed my daughter who was six months old at the time. My kitchen overlooked this window so you could see the street from there. As I picked up a bottle and started walking through the hallway to the room, I noticed a man hunkered over, collar pulled up, fedora pulled down and a cigar in his mouth. What I noticed about him was that he was gray. I pooh-poohed it and thought nothing was going on there because the Apollo Theatre was having a practice that evening of *Tom Sawyer* and the children had been playing in the street prior to that. As I walked the three feet into the room, I noticed the man had disappeared. There was no one at the Apollo. All of the cars were gone.

There was nothing down the street going toward the Bell-Boyd House, and nothing on my street underneath me. The man had vanished into thin air. The next day, I contacted a lady who is actually the town's local ghost hunter, and I mentioned that I had seen something unusual on my street. She laughed, of course, and mentioned that my street just happened to be the most haunted street in Martinsburg due to the Civil War and the activity on the railroad at that time. As I started to describe my experience, she finished my sentence for me and was able to describe this vision back to me. She said, "It looks like you have met Charlie." It turns out that Charlie had once been the manager of the Apollo Theatre when it was still a movie house in the 20s. He took his job very seriously, and evidently Charlie has not left Martin Street. They say that when actors come into the Apollo to practice plays or to put on shows, they will smell cigar smoke. Charlie still monitors all shows. They say that when Charlie worked there that he would stretch his legs by taking a walk around the block and evidently he still likes his fall strolls.

THE MAN IN THE BROWN SUIT
By Ginger Phillips

Around 1960, my husband, Charles, and I and our two daughters (ages 16 & 3) were living in Fayette County, WV. We had been living there about 15 years. There was one family that moved in next door to us. It was just a man (about 50) and his wife, Jenny, who was about 35. She and my 16 year old daughter became good friends. They would trade dresses sometimes. The man's father lived in Morgantown with his two sisters. They would go to Morgantown to see his Father. Many times my daughter would go also and stay all day and sometimes up into the night. Jenny would always see to it that all of the doors were locked and the lights in the house were off. My daughter told me that Jenny was very careful to take care of these things. The houses in their neighborhood were fairly close. Our house was about fifteen feet from theirs with a little fence about 3 feet high between us.

One day they left to go to Morgantown as usual, and I was at my house when I noticed that their lights were on. I thought that was a little strange. I told my daughter when she came back. Everytime they went to Morgantown after that, the lights would come on just about dusk when everyone else would put their lights on. I was getting curious, so I said to my daughter that I believed I would just step over the fence and peep in the window and see who was putting the lights on. My daughter was afraid, and I was too. She said, "Don't go over there, someone may shoot you." So, I never went.

One summer evening after that; my daughters and I decided to take a walk before we went to bed. We walked out the back, into the alley, and up over the little hill. We walked up onto the road and over to the next little road where we would turn left and come up the front way so as to come in our front gate.

We had to pass by the other house before we got to our own. It was almost dark by that time, and we were laughing and talking all at once. When we got right in front of the neighbor's house I said, "Look, the lights are on again." We all looked and after a few minutes I said, "Look, Betty, there's a man in there!"

I wanted to get a little closer, maybe go up on the porch; however, we all stayed in the road. The man that we saw was not much over 5 feet tall, bald, and he was wearing dark clothes. He looked to be about 65 years old and he was holding his pants up to his waist, like he wanted to see whether they fit or not.

Two weeks later, the neighbors went to Morgantown again to bring the man's father home. He was very sick and had to be carried into the house. They gave him a separate room and hired someone to help care for him, but he died shortly after. I believe he was buried in a brown suit. Could he have been the ghost that we saw in the window that night? Maybe.

STRANGE HAPPENINGS
By Linda Moore

I was born and raised in West Virginia. At age 19, I moved to Hilton Head, South Carolina. I was married there, had a child there, and eventually my husband and I bought a home there. It was November 12th, 1991 and it was our four year anniversary. We had a 10 month old son, and had decided that we had outgrown the condominium that we were living in. We were out just driving around that afternoon, and for some reason, I told my husband, Zach, that we should drive down to a friend of ours, Terry Ribette's, home. Terry had left to move to Tennessee.

We called him when we got home. We asked him where the key was, and he told us where it was hidden. We returned to look at it. When we entered into the home, the right side of the house seemed cold to me. There were two bedrooms on the right, a bathroom, an eating area in the center of it, a kitchen. You step down two steps to a second living room. Two steps up and to the right - a dining area, and then a spiral staircase that led up to the loft. On the other side of the house was the master bedroom and bath. There was glass all along the back of the house and a large deck. We decided that we really did like the house and purchased the home.

I continued to have a really strange feeling about the right side of the house, and was always leery about going up to the loft. As a matter of fact, I would not even go up into the loft unless my husband was home. One particular evening, my husband took my young son, and I decided that I was going to brave it and go up into the loft myself. I went up the spiral staircase. As I got to the top, I stood there a moment with my hands on my hips. I switched the light on and said out loud, "I am not afraid." At that point, all five bulbs in the lamp blew out. I slid down the spiral staircase, running to the other side of the house. I slammed the door of the bedroom and picked up the phone. I called a girlfriend and asked her to stay on the line, until my husband got home. When he did, I explained what had happened. He said, "Linda, please don't say these things about this house. I'm sure that it is nothing more than just a fuse, and I am going to show you." My husband picked up my son and we went up the spiral staircase to the loft. We got to the top and Zach turned on the light. The light came on without a problem.

Eventually we decided that we were going to move to Orlando, Florida and rent this house. We rented it to three young banker men. They were of a young age, but very responsible and reasonable. After a year, we returned. They had left a few items in our home. One afternoon they came down to get them. We were sitting there talking when one of the young men said that they thought for a while that the house was haunted. I had never mentioned anything about the lights to them. I said, "What happened to you?" The young man told me that in that one bedroom on the right side of the house, he was there one evening by himself. He was in bed sleeping. He said that it was a light sleep, and that he had heard his door open. It opened all the way then shut. He thought that one of the other roommates had returned and was checking on him. He got up and looked around, went through the entire house and nothing was there. After that, the three men were home one evening, when they heard knocking on the side window where the formal dining room was. There was nothing there. It was heavily wooded and would have been very difficult for someone to have gotten up that far to that particular window. I never told them what I had experienced, but I think they knew that we had known something had gone on.

As time went on, my husband and I started to have trouble in our marriage. It seemed as though that's when more strange happenings started occurring. One evening I was sitting in the living room, and

I could almost feel that something wasn't right. It was about three a.m. and I was getting tired. I went to bed and just dozed off lightly when I heard voices. I couldn't make the voices out. They seemed electronic or computerized. I lay there for a moment. I had a digital clock that was facing me on my bedstand. The green glow that was coming from the display was very eerie and very bright. My cat was running around back and forth without stopping. I had never seen Pepper act that way. As I raised up, the voices stopped. I laid back down, and they started again. When I raised up once more, they stopped again. When I mentioned it to my husband, he casually said, "Linda, I've been hearing these voices for a month. I just thought it was our next door neighbor, Mary, having a party." I said, "Zach, that can't be. Mary's eighty some years old. She's not partying or playing loud music or any of those things."

After that, one evening late, my husband and I had a disagreement. I decided that I would sleep in the bedroom on the right side of the house. I was lying there. My cat came and got into bed. We heard footsteps, padded footsteps, coming across the carpet. I looked up. I looked at the cat. Her eyes were huge. As I looked over to the side of the bed, I saw a greenish mist beside the bed. I jumped out of the bed and ran into our bedroom. When I got into the bed, my husband said, "You heard something, didn't you?"

I decided to tell a neighbor. who told me that she had heard many things happen in the Greenwood Forest area of Hilton Head. She said on one particular night she had heard what appeared to be fighting, terrible fighting, going on in the street. We lived on a dead end street and as I said before it is a heavily wooded area. I had noticed many times, while feeding the raccoons that came up onto the deck, something would appear to scare them off. If you know raccoons, they do not scare easily when there is food. I had six or seven raccoons every evening come for dinner. As I would put the food out, they would stand there and eat. Sometimes they would put themselves up on the glass and sometimes even get into my house. That particular evening, they looked up to the light, stopped, and turned around and all of them left immediately. A short time later they returned to finish their meal. This happened many times. However, on this one night, I was sitting in the chair and heard a knocking. I stood straight up and walked forward about four steps. I turned around slowly looking. All I saw was a cat. The cat appeared to be just frozen, afraid to move. I had fed this cat before, and knew that he was not afraid of anything. I opened the door and I said, "Charlie, what's the matter with you?" Of course, the cat can't talk, but I also realized that the knocking came from much higher up on the door. I brought him in and kept him in the house that night.

As time went on, my husband and I decided to get a divorce. I mentioned to the realtor after we had gotten a contract on the house that her client did indeed have a guest in the home. She became very intrigued by this information. She knew a psychic from England, who was staying in Hilton Head for the summer. Two nights before I moved, I called this woman and asked her what she thought was going on. She told me that it was a nurse from the Civil War Era. She knew that I had been very ill and was trying to help me. It was very sad that I could not understand the voices. She was trying very hard to get through to me. She also said that in the next eighteen months, I would go through a very difficult time in my life. It's been approximately five years, and the woman was very correct in what she told me.

After this conversation, I called the Hilton Head Island Museum. I asked them what had been in the Greenwood Forest area of Hilton Head. They told me, at one point and time during the Civil War, there had been a makeshift hospital. There had also been a prison and trenches. The lady I talked to told me she was a scientist, but that there were supernatural things that went on that could not be explained.

My young son told me, at a later date, that he too had experienced on two different occasions, something or someone appearing to him. Once on the spiral staircase, as his father was going up, a man appeared to come around his father on the staircase towards him. On another occasion, our son who slept with us, woke up in the middle of the night; and the man was standing there beside the bed. I've asked my son many times to tell me the story again. The story never changes.

A few years after I had left, we returned to Hilton Head, my friend and I. I wanted to go down and just take a look at the house. All I could do was look through the window beside the door. It was very strange and very sad. Once again, as I looked through the window, all I could see was a greenish cast covering the living room. It looked very cold and very strange, and once again, very sad. Almost as if it was saying, it was sad that we had left.

Two months before my husband and I split up and I moved back to Charleston from Hilton Head, my best friend of twenty some years called to tell me that her husband, "Hootie," was very ill and possibly not going to live. I immediately decided to come to Charleston. As I was driving to Charleston, a hearse passed me. I knew that "Hootie" had passed away. I became very upset, but there was nothing that I could do except drive on. When I got to Charleston, I asked her if "Hootie" was ok and she said no, that he had indeed, died. We buried "Hootie" on New Year's Eve. That night I had slept in Vickie and "Hootie's" bed because Vickie didn't want to. When I awoke, I smelled very fresh cigarette smoke. "Hootie" was a smoker and had died of lung cancer. When I awoke that morning, I was rather unsettled that someone was being very inconsiderate smoking around her. I went downstairs. We were all sitting talking when Vickie said, "Linda, did you smoke a cigarette this morning?" I knew then that she had smelled the smoke too. I told her that I had not, but that I had smelled it. I said that it was just Hootie letting her know that he was still with her.

On one occasion, I came to my friend's house and said something that "Hootie" would not have approved of. At that point, there was a major stomp, or what would have appeared to have been a stomp over our heads. It was so forceful, that the ceiling tile raised in the kitchen. Vickie has never believed in ghosts. She thought that someone was in the house. She went upstairs, and got her gun. All along, I said that it was just "Hootie." We searched the entire house, and of course, found nothing. What was above the kitchen would have been her dressing room or the guest bedroom. After the complete search of the house, Vickie, again being a non-believer of ghosts or supernatural beings, started to think that there was some merit to all of this. A few nights later, Vickie was in bed with her dog Jake beside the bed, when she heard what sounded like a thud out in the hallway. It sounded as if something were being dragged across the floor.

Eventually, I moved back into the house, and started to hear things myself. One evening, I was upstairs by myself and Vickie was downstairs with a guest. I heard what sounded like marbles being dropped and rolling across a marble floor. I thought that she had dropped something downstairs, and she thought that I had broken something upstairs. After that, one evening I went up the steps into my bedroom. On the steps and it was as if there were an electrical buzzing sound right above my head. The farther I got up the steps and into the bedroom, the louder the noise. I asked Vickie to come up and see if she could hear it, and she could. That evening she had a guest again. He is a very logical person. He came up and he heard it. He said it must be something electrical in the attic. We both went into the attic and there was nothing.

On a sunny Sunday afternoon, and I was talking on the phone to a friend. There is a room in the house which we refer to as the blue room because there is a very old canopy bed with a blue canopy top. The bed itself is well over a hundred years old and belongs to my family. I had always felt that something about the bed created these occurrences. I heard the closet door in the room slam shut. The person on the phone heard it too. He came to the house and found nothing. Many of these instances that happened did not seem to scare me.

Another time I was sitting in my room with my cat, and Vickie's dog, Jake. Out of the blue room, we heard women's voices. Once again I could not understand what was being said. My cat got up, walked over to the room, dare not entering, only standing in the doorway. She stood there for a few minutes then came back to lay down.

I can think of only one time when I got a little bit afraid. I was in my bed, and heard footsteps coming up to the side of the bed. I jumped up and got my foot tangled in the bedsheets. After I got untangled, I ran into Vickie's room and jumped into the bed with her. She asked me if I had heard something. I said that I did and that I was definitely sleeping with her.

It is rather strange though, that Vickie decided to sell her home approximately two years ago. All of the houses that have gone on the market up and down the street, have sold in a relatively short amount of time. Vickie's home is quite large, and she has it priced very reasonably; but for some reason, it has never sold. Never even had an offer. It makes me wonder if Vickie was meant to stay in this house with those who love her from beyond.

Once, in the summer of 2000, when I was staying at Vickie's house, I was laying on the sofa in my bedroom. I was just dozing off when I smelled a horrible odor. I thought that my cat had come in and made a terrible mess. I began to look for it, but didn't find anything. About a week later, I was again lying on the couch, and the same smell enters the room. I searched again and once again found nothing. Two weeks later, my son and I were lying on the bed watching TV when the smell returned - a terrible smell. I asked my son if he had possibly done that and he said no. After he went to sleep, I stayed there watching TV and the smell returned. This time, I had had it. I told the ghost, "I know that you are here, and I am getting very tired of this odor you are making. Please Stop!" I have never smelled the odor again.

It seems as though no matter where I go, or where I live, I seem to come upon strange happenings in the spirit world. About a month ago, I rented a home. The home itself is a beautiful little Cape Cod style home, red in color, with a beautiful little yard. When I first entered into the home it was already rented and seemed all cozy and warm and nice. A family was living in it, and they said that it was a great home, one that they had enjoyed greatly. I looked so forward to moving in. It seemed that there was one delay after another, but finally I could move my things in. Vickie's brother said that he would move in and paint the house. I decided to stay at Vickie's while he was doing it. Her brother got ill and couldn't finish the work, so my son Zach and I continued to live with Vickie. One evening we went to check on her Vickie's brother. He was lying on the couch sleeping. Vickie and I were sitting there talking. We heard in my bedroom (which was the attic) very heavy footsteps walking across the floor. Vickie thinking that someone or something had gotten in, went racing up the stairs. I had never been afraid of ghosts myself, but something stopped me that evening. I stopped at the bottom of the steps. Vickie searched the entire attic and the storage room. A few days later, Vickie and a friend of hers went back to the house to check on her brother. They went up to my bedroom and were sitting there talking when they heard the bedroom door open. They heard someone walking up the steep stair case. They stopped and listened and then went over to look. Nobody was there. A few days later, I went out to feed the cat. Vickie's brother had moved out. I had left the lights on, the lamp in the living room and one in the bedroom for the cat. The next morning, I walked in the house to feed Pepper, only to find the lights turned off. I have yet to move into the house. So far, only Matthew and my cat have lived there. I am a little leery of this one, and I don't know why. I guess that it is the unknown that people are always afraid of. People keep asking me if it is a good ghost or a bad ghost. That remains to be seen.

MOMMY'S STORIES
By Glenna Hager

Story One

This story took place when my mom was still at home, before she married. She had a little brother who had an illness, we know it as polio today, because his legs were drawn up. She said that they were walking home from church when she saw a vision of a little casket floating down the creek. When they turned to cross the bridge to where they lived, it turned up on its end and vanished. When they went inside, she said you could smell death. It was a warm night, and yet it was so cold in her brother's room. She said that she felt a breeze pass by her. They called a doctor, who came and pronounced him dead. Mommy said the vision was to let her know that the Lord was going to take him home.

Everyone said that he was such a perfect and beautiful child. They said when he was a baby that he would not live to be an adult because he was too perfect. God would want to take him home before that.

Story Two

This story begins when I was 9 years old. Mom was always afraid of thunderstorms. Whenever the lightning and thunder would start, my mom would put us in one room with a light and she would sit in one of the bedrooms where she could see us. It was during one of these storms that she saw this thing.

Every so often, she would raise the blind on the window to see if the storm was blowing over. This storm was so bad, it just kept on and on with the lightning flashing every few seconds. Mom didn't know what it was she saw. She said it had a peaked head and it maybe arms. The whole time it was at the window it didn't lightning one time.

I remember that when daddy came home from the night shift at the saw mill, she told him about it and said that she did not want to stay the night in that house. Daddy got all of us up and we walked to my grandmother's house about two miles away. When we returned home the next day we saw that there were scratches from the window all the way around the house and there were places in the dirt that looked like a broom handle had been stuck in the ground all the way around the house and up the hill. Mommy never mentioned this incident again, but she insisted that daddy find us another place to live. She experienced one more strange thing before we moved. When I was little, we didn't have running water in the house; so, when mom washed dishes she would pour the dish water in a kettle for daddy to put in his pig feed. Anyway, mom poured it in and it was so full that it would not hold another drop. She heard a noise in the kitchen. When she went into the kitchen, the kettle was on its side but the water had not spilled. It was as if it was frozen. The back door had a wooden latch which you had to use two hands to open or close. When she saw the kettle on its side, the lock started spinning around and around very quickly. When mommy went over to lock it, it was just as hard as ever to turn.

One time, when I was playing outside, I saw a man in the woods. I told mom and she went out to look for the man to see what he wanted, but he was gone. Mom told me to get ready and we would go to grandma's. While we were walking a car pulled up and the same man that I had seen in the woods earlier told us to get in. Mom wouldn't accept a ride with a stranger, and said no thank you. He insisted but mom told him that we were going right here. We started across the bridge and he left. We didn't even know the people in the house that we were going to - but thank God there was a house there. Who knows what might have happened.

Story Three

This story begins with a house that I guess really was haunted. Everyone who had lived in this house said that they had heard things. Mom said that when she and daddy lived there something would pull the covers off them at night, but if she put them back they would stay put. Daddy still worked at the saw mill and he would bring home slats to burn and keep them warm. One night, Mom said that she heard daddy throw down the wood. She got up to let him in and got right back into bed. Daddy didn't come in. She heard him walk up onto the porch, and he still didn't come in.

She closed the door. After a while, daddy did come home. Mom said she heard him lay down the wood and she hollered to ask if it was him and he said yes, so she opened the door again. This time, she saw a man coming through our gate. He was wearing black pants and a white shirt. He kept walking and mom said, "Everett, speak to him." Daddy didn't say anything because he didn't see anyone. Mom said that when daddy went down the steps this "man" walked right behind him and when they got to the corner of the house, he vanished. Daddy swears he didn't see anything or anyone.

My grandparents had also lived in the house and they and other relatives said that they have seen and heard things that made no sense. They could hear a baby crying, they saw a stain in the corner of the kitchen which looked like a blood stain. They claimed a girl had been shot there and they could not get the stain cleaned up. Everyone who lived there had tried.

My mom's sister and her husband had lived there for a while. She said that after supper one evening she had cleaned up the kitchen and gone to the living room. Later, she heard someone walking around. She said it sounded like they had nails in the bottom of their shoes and they kept pulling the rug when they walked. Then, she heard this sound like the china cabinet being turned over and everything in it breaking. When it got quiet, they went in to see. They turned on the light and everything was just as it had been.

No one ever knew why this house would not let anyone rest in it. Some people said that the house was built on graves from when the Indians had lived there. When someone would move in, it would start again until they moved out. The house was located on a hill in Droudy, WV, but it has since been torn down. We hope that whoever was buried there is now at peace.

Story Four

Mom and daddy were living in their house on Camp Creek. Mommy never talked much about this place, except that she and daddy had heard something upstairs. They would leave the light on upstairs and they wouldn't hear anything. One night, daddy said he was going to sleep up there and see what was making the noise. He tied a string around his finger and attached it to the light cord. When he pulled the string the light didn't come on. He also had a ball bat up there. He said he felt a presence on the bed. Daddy started hitting this thing. Daddy finally went to sleep and when he woke up there was hair on the end of the bat and hair on the bed which looked like some kind of an animal. My brother slept up there all of the time and he said he could feel something on his bed like soft footprints. He was never afraid and said it was there for a reason, so why be afraid.

Again, in this same house there was another occurrence. One day, mom said she and daddy were there alone and they heard a noise on the outside of the house near the window. They looked outside and the power line was shaking hard from the pole to the house. There was no one there and the weather was fine. Mommy and daddy were never afraid either because they said they never hurt anyone.

I would like to dedicate this story to the memory of my parents, Everett and Hessie Bowman.

AMANDA'S ANGEL
By Amanda Winnell

Amanda Winnell was thirteen at the time and she lives in South Charleston.

I met someone at Derrick's Rollarena in North Charleston. A girl just approached me as a friendly gesture. The girl said that I looked upset. I said that I was not upset, just tired. The girl said her name was Dawn and that she was eighteen. She had blond hair and light eyes and was dressed like any other teenager. After Dawn had been talking to me for a while, she informed me that she had been watching me. She said that she was not a stalker, she was my angel. Dawn said my father had been worried about me because I had been getting into trouble at school and arguing with my mother. I had never seen this girl before in my life. Dawn said that this is probably the first and last time that I would ever see her because she traveled around the world.

Dawn knew facts she could not have known because she didn't know me. She knew how old my dad was when he died (46), his name, that he worked for the South Charleston Police Department for 10 yrs, that he was at work when he died, and that he was in a computer room alone when he died. Dawn then said she was not playing a joke on me and that she would prove it. Dawn told me to cup my hands together and concentrate. She then cupped her hands over mine and there was a quick gust of cold air from her hands into mine. Up until that point, I was very skeptical, but after that, I believed. She said if I was scared or lonely to remember she was there to guide me and that everything would be ok. Oh, and on that night, I didn't see Dawn come in, nor did I see her leave.

Dawn also said she had once been a living person, but she was just appearing in the flesh now. She said she had been with her boyfriend, and they had been engaged; but he had to go away to war.

My boyfriend was with me this night, but he was mad at me. All of my friends were going outside. Dawn said, "I know he's kind of mad at you right now, but I want you to go outside and find him and if he comes up to you and hugs you (which I have a feeling he will), then he is the one for you; but if you go out there and you have to go up to him, then he will not be for you." When I went out there, he came right up to me and hugged me.

I have noticed other times when I thought that maybe Dawn was near. A radio will be on, then automatically turn off. Doors will close. I will roll over in bed and see a dark figure sitting next to it, and I know that it is Dawn. I even had something happen the night that I met Dawn. I was curling my hair in my mom's room when the door slammed.

There was no one there and the windows were closed.

THE ESTEP FAMILY GUARDIAN
By Chris Estep

My name is Chris Estep and I live in Dunbar. I have had some strange occurences in my home. The most specific incident I remember was on New Year's Day. I was waiting on my husband to get home from work and was taking clothes to the drier. While Rob was at work, I heard the telephone ring. I heard the kitchen chair scoot out and footsteps going to the telephone. I assumed that Rob was already home form work, but he usually calls first to see if I need anything from the store. I went upstairs calling his name but he was not there. When I checked the answering machine, it was Rob who had called. That was probably the most spooky, but it did let us know something was going on.

This spirit has actually touched me. I felt her pat me on the back. At that point, I was aware that we did have something in the house. I asked her not to touch me like that because it scared me. We are aware that there is something here, because there are always footsteps coming up from the recreation room. In the morning, after I have worked night shift, I will pull the bedroom door shut without totally closing it; and you can hear the footsteps and see the shadow under the door. We are pretty used to that. She's slept on my bed before. I can feel the weight on the bed and the indentation at the bottom of the mattress. I have asked her not to do that as well.

Rob hasn't had contact with her in about a year. We do feel cold spots in the house though.

Our neighbor, Ray, will get goosebumps all over his body just standing there until he moves out of that area. It is not cold, like a normal cold, but we all get goosebumps. The minute I back out of it, they're gone.

On New Year's Eve, Ray came upstairs to use the bathroom. He was in the bathroom when he felt someone watching him. He turned around and not exactly saw, but knew. He said, "This is your house, these are your people. I'm using your bathroom, and then I'll be on my way." He had not been drinking either. He knew that there was someone there and he just apologized for coming up and bothering them. There is definitely something up here, but it does not seem harmful.

Rob saw the spirit about a year ago. Rob was laying in bed filling out a survey for my son's school that we both had to do. He caught a glimpse of something out of the corner of his eye. He said that it was a figure with long, dark hair, and what looked to be a white dress or gown. She just turned around and came back up the hall because she saw him look. That is the only time he had ever seen her. She has passed by him a few times because he has felt a breeze go by.

I like Sylvia Brown, the psychic. Anytime I have an astrology or a Sylvia Brown book out, I can expect increased activity. There was a book out one night when Connie Miller and another friend of mine were laughing and joking about our horoscopes, when the lights started dimming and went out. So we lit a white candle, and the flame would go up and down by itself. The Millers were here one evening and were getting ready to leave. I had a flower arrangement on the table, and all of a sudden one flower just drooped down to the table. That really scared us. The Millers were trying to leave and the door wouldn't open. It was not locked, the doorknob just wouldn't turn.

I know a woman named Becky Ratliff who reads cards and drives the spirits away. Becky asked me what was going on at my house before I even had a chance to say anything. She told me to watch over my son. When Jeremy was little he went through the storm glass door. He could have been impaled, but there was not a scratch on him. She said this spirit protects you but fire really bothers her. She watches over the house and makes sure that it is safe. It has gotten to be a joke that when we leave we say watch over the house. Becky said that this being has taken the form of an older woman so as not to frighten me. The one Ron experienced was younger. I have felt her touch and presence on the bed. My grandmother died when she was thirty two, so we started to call the spirit, Lottie, but we quickly learned not to call it that. There will be a lot of increased activity if you call her that. This spirit is supposed to be watching over me, and I truly feel that she is. I have no problem with her being here.

This past Halloween, Jeremy and I were sitting on the couch and I was helping him with his homework. Jeremy had to make a word search having to do with Halloween. He had mentioned the word phantom and the light automatically turned itself off. He hasn't said it since.

I feel that there is only one spirit here. Becky says that there are many, but only the one feels comfortable enough to reveal herself to us.

GHOSTLY GUEST, OR
HOW I MET MY FATHER IN LAW
by Karla Arveson

I never knew my husband's father. He passed away about 40 years ago when my husband, Robert, was 10 or 11 years old.

In 1986, we moved into a house we built behind his mother's, on property that has been in my husband's family since the late 20s or early 30s.

One afternoon I was sitting in the living room watching TV. I had been home from work less than an hour. Out of the corner of my eye, I saw someone coming out of the bathroom.

I turned my head to look, and looked directly into the eyes of a man I had never seen before. Before I could even blink, he "poofed" away into my son's bedroom directly across from the bathroom.

Michael was four or five at the time. I went into Michael's room, which had become much colder than the rest of the house. I somehow knew it was Bruno, my husband's father. I spoke in a whisper saying, "Hello...," told him I was glad he'd come to visit and that he was welcome anytime. I straightened Michael's covers and went back to watch TV.

Minutes later, Michael came running out of his room crying, "Mommy! Mommy! There's a ghost in my room!" I got him settled on the sofa and back to sleep and then went back into Mike's room and whispered again to Bruno, "I'm sorry Mike got scared, he's just a little boy, I hope you'll visit again," or words to that effect.

He was clearly visible, wearing a plaid flannel shirt, I think was green. Although I remember all these details, he was also kind of transparent. I could clearly see the doorframe and wall behind (through) him.

A few years later, I saw the back of a man's calf and heel of his boot going past my kitchen doorway into my bedroom where my husband was sleeping. I knew it was Bruno again, and I knew why he was there. Earlier that night, my sister, our two brothers and I had taken our kids to the circus. My husband had refused to go with us. Bruno came to tell him that he wasn't a part of Robert's childhood because he had passed away. What was Robert's excuse?

I have never seen Bruno again, although I have sensed his presence a few other times. I feel blessed to have been able to see him, and would love to have the pleasure of seeing other family and friends who have crossed over.

RETURN FOR A DRINK
by Susan Pettit

My father, Jim Hash, enjoyed being outside working in the fresh air. He always had a garden and he liked to tinker with Gravely tractors. He also had a large yard to keep up.

After a couple of hours of hard work, he would come in the back door, go to the kitchen sink, turn on the water and let it run for a minute and then get himself a glass of water. He would stand at the sink drinking his water looking out the kitchen window into the yard. When finished, he would then go down the hall to use the bathroom. Now "filled up and emptied" he would head back outside. This was a daily ritual in our home.

After his death, several family members started telling of the same unexplained experience. They were usually in the house alone and would hear the back door open and footsteps in the kitchen. Then, they would hear the sound of running water. After several minutes the commode would flush. Several of us even would run to the bathroom just in time to see the water swirling around. We knew that my dad was paying us a visit and no one in the family was afraid. In fact, it was more of a comfort knowing he was around.

After my mother died in 1993, things were pretty quiet around the house - no running water or commodes flushing. Then my daughter blessed us with 2 grandchildren. The first grandchild, Jordan, would often ask her mother if her Grandma Ethel was coming to play with her today. My daughter would walk by Jordan's room and hear her talking to my mother as if she was playing with her.

Then Alex was born. When he was just over a year old, he started telling us that he was talking with his Grandpa Jim. One day I was letting Alex play in that same sink that Jim would stand by and drink his water and I could tell by the look on Alex's face that he was seeing someone. No one was there but me. Alex started talking up a storm to his Grandpa Jim. We have enjoyed the visits from our parents and look forward to the day when we can really see them face to face and talk about their visits to us.

THE BELL WITCH
by Dennis Deitz

> **3C 38**
> **BELL WITCH**
>
> To the north was the farm of John Bell, an early, prominent settler from North Carolina. According to legend, his family was harried during the early 19th century by the famous Bell Witch. She kept the household in turmoil, assaulted Bell, and drove off Betsy Bell's suitor. Even Andrew Jackson who came to investigate, retreated to Nashville after his coach wheels stopped mysteriously. Many visitors to the house saw the furniture crash about them and heard her shriek, sing, and curse.

While visiting my granddaughter near Nashville at Greenbrier TN, her husband, Max Carter and I made a trip to see the site and home of John Bell and the famous poltergeist called the Bell Witch. We visited the Bell Witch museum which is open to the public, took pictures of the historical roadside marker as well as the tall memorial dedicated to the Bell family.

This 200 year old story tells of the John Bell family and any friends or neighbors who befriended them as being harassed and even physically tortured by what they called the Bell witch who finally sent John Bell to his death.

This famous story was investigated by many well known persons including then General Andrew Jackson who left after one night saying that he would rather face an entire British army than the Bell witch who was also called Katie. Katie also made many predictions concerning future historic events which came true.

We also talked to many people in the Nashville area.
Everyone seemed to know about the Bell Witch or spirit or Katie as she was also called. Though, if you had a hundred
people there, they would each have a different version of this story.

About a month after this visit I returned to interview more people. Bo Adams is a collector of everything he can find concerning the Bell Witch and has a collection of 50 books and articles on this subject. In his collection is a quote from one of the books saying, "John Bell was the only known case whose death was caused by a witch or a spirit."

The story of how John Bell died was that he suffered in agony. The doctor was called. He found a bottle of liquid which had been given to or forced on him somehow. When the Doctor gave a cat this same liquid, it died in agony. The Doctor was never able to determine what the liquid was.

ST. FRANCIS GHOST
By Sheila Scott

Some years ago, I was a nurse at the St. Francis Hospital in Charleston, WV. One day another nurse and I entered the restroom together. I saw a little white headed lady enter the bathroom just ahead of us. When we got into the restroom, I couldn't see the lady. I checked both the stalls, and I still did not see her. Puzzled, I asked the other nurse if she had seen anyone enter the restroom in front of us. She said, "Sure, a little old lady with white hair."

I asked, "Where is she now?"

She answered, "I have no idea where she could have gone."

As we came out of the restroom the bell sounded which means that someone had died. It was the little old lady with white hair who had just died in her room.

THE FAMILY CURSE
By Candice Lynch

My dad used to live in a haunted house. it was a rental, and many families lived in it over time. Every family who had lived there had the same strange and terrible thing happen to them. One person out of each family would mysteriously die. Well, there was a friend of my grandpa's who lived with them. One day he was sitting out on the porch and he had a heart attack. Also, the girls would lock their doors at night, fold their clothes, and lay them on their dressers. In the morning they were scattered all over the room. Candles would float in mid air. Windows would slam at certain times of the night.

The scariest thing that my grandma ever told me was that one night when she got up to use the restroom, she saw a figure of someone. She said, "In the name of the Father, the Son, and the Holy Ghost, leave here." It did, however, she never forgot the figure's face. She said it was the most hideous thing she had ever seen.

THE DEVIL'S FIRE
By Candice Lynch

This is a true story told to me by my great grandmother. Her great aunt lived on Greenbrier Mountain in White Sulphur Springs. She had just given birth to twins. Her husband was a moonshiner, and was away at the time.

She was a devout Christian and one night, while rocking her children to sleep, she saw a hideous creature walk up her steps in chains. He had a hollow face. She said, "You're a pretty tough looking customer." He then disappeared.

The next day, she went to take lunch to her husband. While she was gone, the house burned down with both children inside. Was the creature's appearance an omen of death?

COMFORTING SPIRITS IN THE CUMBERLAND PLATEAU
By Suzette Roberts

Sparta is a small farming community located in mid-central Tennessee. It is nestled in the foothills of the Smoky Mountains. It is there that my story takes place. My grandparents, Sallie and Leon Dodson met, married, raised their family of six children and eventually died in Sparta. My mom is the fifth of their children. After graduating high school, mom left home and married my father in Atlanta, however all of our holidays and summer vacations were spent in Sparta with our grandparents, aunts, uncles, and nine first cousins.

In 1975, in preparation for retirement, my parents bought an existing farm that had once belonged to a man I had only heard called "Doc" Phillips. It was a small three-bedroom wood framed house and was sufficient for their needs at the time. This house provided a place for us to stay when visiting Tennessee without imposing on our relatives anymore. Uncles and cousins leased out the 56 acres and cared for the property when my parents were not there.

Sadly, my grandmother, Sallie, was diagnosed with inoperable cancer in the spring of 1976 and the family was told she would not live much longer. My mother went to Tennessee and had a hospital bed brought into her farmhouse where all the family took turns tending to Granny until she died a few weeks later. Many of the family continued to come back to my parent's house dropping by food and staying to speak with Granny. Just before her death, she called as much of the family that was there into her room and told them she did not want anyone to be sad or grieving her death. Granny was a religious woman and rarely missed a church service. She said that she knew she was going to a better place and would be happy there and she wanted everyone else to be happy for her too. She did not want anyone to mourn her death, especially her grandchildren. Granny died not long after this conversation with her family.

The night of the viewing, the funeral home was filled with family and friends. Family had gone to the funeral home and had spent an hour alone before it was opened to the public. Oddly, most all of the twelve grandchildren there were within a six year range of each other's age and were all teenagers at the time that Granny died. As teenagers do, no matter what the circumstances, four of them migrated together and had gone outside on the porch and were talking. The conversation lightened and laughter drifted from the group. One of our aunts came outside and became irritated with the youth's seeming lack of respect at the time of her mother's death. She told the youths that if they could not act "like somebody" and be more respectful, they could just go to the house. As teenagers do, they became offended by her reactions and went in and told their respective mothers that they would, indeed, leave and go back to my parent's house.

As this small group of teenagers arrived at the house, they decided they would eat. The kitchen was full of food that had been brought to the house by friends and relatives. They busied themselves digging through the refrigerator and peeking into bowls on the table and counters. Lighthearted conversation filled the kitchen as they laughed and joked with each other. A noise was suddenly heard from the front bedroom. A noise loud enough that the group felt that it should be investigated. They decided that they should all go together. As they left the kitchen there was another loud noise coming from the front bedroom where our grandmother had died.

Slowly they advanced into the bedroom. There in this room standing beside the bed where she had died stood Sallie Dodson. Granny spoke to four of her grandchildren, and told them that she did not want them to be upset about the chastising they had gotten from their aunt. She was very happy where she was and she wanted them to be happy too, as they were at the funeral home. She did not want them to be sad and crying and mourning after her but to continue on with their lives and to tell everyone that she was happy. She smiled at all of them and simply faded away.

My parents returned home to Maryland shortly after Granny was laid to rest, but three weeks later my Dad returned to Tennessee to do some work on the roof of the small farmhouse. Spring had come by then and he was up on the roof doing some simple repairs. It was a warm day and he was preparing to come down off the ladder when he looked down on the porch. Sitting in the porch swing sat Granny. It seemed so normal since many times she visited when my parents came down and Dad thought nothing of it at the moment. Granny looked up at Dad and asked if he would like a glass of tea. "Sure," Dad replied, "I'll be right down." Granny got up and went into the house. A moment passed and Dad realized that it could not have been her. He descended the ladder, went onto the porch and into the house. No one else was in the house, but a glass of fresh iced tea was sitting on the kitchen table.

A quarter of a mile from the original farmhouse, my parents built a new modern house on their land and retired there. My two sisters moved to Tennessee at the same time and Penny moved into the original farmhouse with her husband. In February of 1982, she gave birth to Waymon Andrew Allen. He was the first of my parents grandchildren and would have been the first great-grandchild, had either set of our grandparents been living. My sister was greatly bothered by the fact that our grandparents would never see their great-grandchildren and thought of this often. She named her firstborn after both of his grandfathers as a tribute to them. When she came home from the hospital, she and her husband stayed with my mother for a couple of days.

One afternoon, she laid Andy in a bassinet at the foot of the bed and laid down for a much-needed nap. She awakened because she felt that someone was looking at her. When she opened her eyes our Dad's father, Jesse was standing at the foot of the bed, wearing a suit and holding a Bible in his hand. This in itself would not be unusual but our grandfather had died in 1980 of a massive heart attack. Penny sat up and asked what he was doing there. He smiled at her and told her that this was a beautiful baby and that she should take good care of it. He knew that she had been worrying so about him seeing this baby and that now she could quit worrying and get her rest. He turned and walked out of our parent's bedroom and turned down the hall. Penny turned back the covers and jumped out of bed to follow him, but when she looked down the hall, he was gone.

My parents had a full basement built in this house and finished off half of the basement as a large family room. Most of their time was spent in this room. Many times when friends and family would come to the house, they might knock and softly enter without waiting for a reply. They would walk down the bare-wood hall calling out for someone until the family could be located. On several occasions, my parents would be with visitors in the family room, laughing and talking when someone would enter the house. They would hear someone walking down the hall, sounding as if he or she were walking with a cane, enter the bathroom and flush the commode. Many times they called out a greeting, but no one replied or came back down the hall. Upon going upstairs, there would be no one there. The house had been built one-quarter of a mile from the road with a gravel drive to the house. The closest neighbor was one-half mile on either side. Their property backed up to connecting property that belonged to my uncle who grazed cattle in this field. In his field stood the rundown ruins of an old homestead consisting only of a broken down frame and chimney.

One sunny summer day after the unseen visitor had walked down the hall several times, my mother was working out in the yard. Upon turning and facing the field, she saw a man standing in the field on the other side of the fence. He was leaning upon the fence, resting his elbow on one of the posts. Leaning against the post was a cane. The man appeared to be in his late sixties to early seventies and had a long beard. My mother described him to be dressed in what was called Lindsay woolen; cloth that had been spun on a spinning wheel and made in a style of clothing of an era long since past. She spoke to the gentleman, but he never replied and continued to just stare at her. She put down her shovel and removed her gardening gloves but when she looked up, he had vanished. She looked up and down the fence row but he was just gone. A short time later our uncle decided to tear down the old homestead. He burned the ruins and tore down the chimney. From that point in time, the unseen visitor never entered my parent's home again. Could he have been the owner of the home and the visitor at the fence? My parents thought so, but no one ever knew.

Sometimes stories are told that we find hard to believe and sometimes the reader just doesn't want to believe them. But, when stories are told by the people you know and trust the most, it is hard not to believe.

Before composing this story, I contacted my relatives to be sure of the accuracy of the facts. They maintain that these odd events occurred. My sister said that when things such as this happen, they aren't easy to forget. I agree.

WHY ME LORD?
By Diana Linn Miller

In 1945, the war was over and my dad was finally coming home. My mom found out that she couldn't have children. She had always wanted them, so the next best thing was to adopt. My parents told me at an early age, how they picked me out over the other babies and it made me feel very special. Mom seemed to relish the memory of me taking hold of her finger when she first saw me. She said she knew then that I was the one she wanted. They said that I cried quite often for several weeks, but I finally settled down and became their pride and joy.

My parents were told at the time they found me in the shelter that I had a congenital heart defect which was terminal and that surgery was out of the question. The doctors said that I probably would not reach my teens. That didn't stop my mom. She said she wanted to care for me as long as the Lord would allow them to have me. That is real love and I will always be grateful.

Between the ages of four and seven, I can remember the times that going to the doctor meant heart checkups which included a very large machine hovering over me, Being a small child, that machine looked so scary. I guess it was like some type of x-ray machine, but whatever it was, the results were never very promising. I was too young to understand that life would be very short for me, and there never seemed to be any hope that something could ever be done for this problem.

I also enjoyed going to Parkersburg, WV to visit my grandparents on my mom's side of the family. My grandfather had been a store owner for years. He had been very sick for a long time and had finally become bed ridden. One day my mom's cousin asked if mom and I would accompany her on a trip to speak with my grandfather about his salvation, because death was nearing and he wasn't ready spiritually. I remember standing at the bed when our cousin was praying for my grandfather, and he told us that he had made things right with God and that he would like for the Lord to give him at least three days to be a witness to others when they came to visit. The Lord granted his wish, and three days later, my grandfather died.

On the way back home from praying with grandpa, our cousin asked mom if she would object to stopping by to see her pastor and have him to pray for my heart problem. I remember getting there and seeing a man dressed in bibbed overalls, working in a garden. After visiting for a short while, the preacher asked me to come over and sit beside him. He asked if I loved Jesus, and I said that I did. He then asked if I believed that Jesus could heal my heart. He began praying for me. My mom said it was like a lightning bolt hit her when he was praying. He told mom that she should take me back to the heart specialist to see if any change had taken place. He said that he was not going to get her hopes up, but he felt that something good was going to happen.

A few days later, we went to the specialist. The doctor listened to my heart and did his usual routine checkup. After he was through, he looked at my mom and said " I'm not a religious man, but something has taken place that I cannot explain. There is no sign of any heart problem." I don't think my mom could even speak at that point. I was healed, but to this day, I ask "why me Lord?"

Many many years later I was invited to a birthday party in Oak Hill with my friends, Charlie and Betty. Oak Hill was the town my natural family was supposed to be from. My mom had also told me the name I was given at birth, and that I had siblings. I never tried to find my family because I was afraid that my adoptive parents might feel that I wasn't satisfied with them. As I grew older, I began wondering about my siblings. I figured my real parents may not be interested in knowing that I was alive or want to know anything about me, but every time I would see someone who resembled me, I would wonder if we could be related.

At the birthday party I was introduced to a lady who was working on a family tree. Charlie told her about the fact that I may have family in the Oak Hill area. As I stood up to leave, she said "By the way, I happen to have a newspaper in my car that has an obituary with the same name. Maybe if you look up the names listed as family, you could locate them and they may be able to help you in your search".

Betty commented that we should stop by the funeral home to inquire if anyone had information for me. I told her that there was no way I would go to a funeral home dressed in blue jeans and ask questions to people in mourning, but that is exactly what we did.

I reluctantly followed Charlie to the door. Charlie asked if we could speak with a director. I was so nervous and so embarrassed. Charlie looked at me and told me to tell him the purpose of our intrusion. I nervously told him that I was trying to find a lead to someone that might know something of my adoption. He was so nice, and he told us to wait there because he had someone he wanted us to meet. A lady followed him to the office and he introduced her to us. She got all excited and was anxious for us to meet her family. Her brother was the deceased, but our being there did not bother her in the least. She asked if I would like to meet her mother. She was the same age as my parents, and I was so hoping that maybe she would know something about my family. Her mother was the sweetest looking little lady and as we were introduced, she took my hand. I explained why I was there, and I began telling her what my name had been at birth and that my family was from the Oak Hill area. She was thinking back, but couldn't remember anyone. The daughter was so disappointed. She stated that she wished we could be sisters. She was willing to adopt me right then and there so that we could be related. I couldn't imagine anyone being so nice and accommodating to a person who had the nerve to walk into a funeral home during a time of sorrow. I thanked them for their time, and that little sweet lady squeezed my hand and said she wished she could help me.

I noticed that the car was not where it was when Rod let us out. We looked around, and another sister whom we met, had brought their brother, Wayne, to meet us. He was also working on a family tree and he wanted to meet me and give him information to help in his search. That made me happy, because that way I would be able to have contact with someone from that wonderful family we had just met.

As we were driving back home, I could not get those people off my mind. Betty commented that she had some kind of strange feeling that kept haunting her, but she could not understand why.

I then contacted a lady at an agency who was very friendly. She told me that she would be more than glad to help me, but if my family had never tried to locate me, she would not be at liberty to give me any information. If my family had been told that I was terminal at birth, they probably would think I had died shortly after birth and would have no reason to search for me. She said she would try to find out something and get back in touch with me. When she called me back I was quite shocked. She told me that I had four siblings, and I almost fell off my chair. I said to her, "You found me!?" She chuckled, and said that she had the information before her, but that she couldn't give me any names because there was no record of anyone trying to locate me. I was so disappointed. She then asked if there was anything that I could tell her that might help her in disclosing something that otherwise would be against policy. I told her about the trip we had made to Oak Hill and the people we had met at the funeral home, but that was all I had. She asked if I could give her any names of the people at the funeral home who were related to the deceased and also what his name was. I told her the name listed in the obituary. She said, "What?" I told her about Lori and Wayne. There was silence for a moment and she then asked if I could find out the name of their mother. All at once, that feeling I had when I met Lori, was there again. I couldn't remember their mother's name, but I remembered the name of the funeral home and the director. I was shaking by that time, and I told her that I would call the director and get the name. She said she would tell me one thing, that my real mother's name began with an "A". I knew I shouldn't make a long distance call from work, but at this stage, I didn't care! I dialed the phone number and the director answered the phone. I asked him if he could tell me the name of the deceased man's mom. He told me that her name was Arbutus. My hands were shaking so badly, I could hardly dial the number, but when I reached the lady I had been talking with, I told her the name given to me. She said, " Honey, you just found your family." I will never be able to express the feeling I had when she said that to me. A fellow employee came running to my desk when she heard me crying, and when I told her what I had just found out, she began crying too.

I called Charlie to tell him what had just happened. I said "I held hands with my real mom and didn't know it". He was in shock as much as I was. That evening, Rod and I went to Charlie's house. I wanted Charlie to call Wayne for me while he would still be in Oak Hill. I wasn't ready to explain to anyone who might answer the phone as to why we were calling. We were not in a position at that time to say anything about what had happened that day. Charlie spoke with Wayne and told him that he had called on my behalf and then he handed the phone to me. Boy! I didn't know what to say, so I just told him that I had something very important to talk with him about. He said he would give me a call as soon as he returned home to Virginia. I could tell by the serious tone of his voice, that he may have figured out what was going on.

A couple of days later, Charlie called to tell me he had contacted a judge. I told the judge what had taken place and asked if there was any way I could obtain my original birth certificate or information about my adoption. We were surprised when he told his secretary to give him a paper to sign. It was addressed to the 'Clerk of Court' and requested that my adoption file be opened and that I have access to all the information contained in that file. I was handed a simple piece of paper that held the key to my past. Most people struggle to obtain any information they can find to help locate their family. I just walked into a judge's office and within minutes, I had everything I needed. Once the 'Clerk of Courts' office had opened the files and placed copies in my hand, I found out all about my natural family and my adoptive parents.

As I read those adoption papers, I was in awe. There, before me, was the name of my natural father. I quickly looked him up in the phone directory. What was I going to say, once I made the call? I was told that he had passed away, but that he had a son by the name of Tommy. She gave me the number, and I nervously called him. I explained to him what I had just found out, and although I knew it would be a shock for him, I felt that this was a very important matter, especially for me. Tommy was very understanding as we talked and he told me to please come and visit soon. He was recovering from recent open heart surgery and wasn't doing very well.

The next evening, my brother, Wayne, called. I told him the information I had obtained and he was not surprised. Now, all of a sudden, it was like the sky had opened up and was pouring one miracle after another down on me.

A couple of weeks later, I went to visit Tommy and his wife, Betty. As soon as I walked up on the porch, Tommy came out to greet us. His first words to us were "I knew you were one of us because you look just like our family".

Finally, I was ale to talk to my mother, and it was the most wonderful conversation in the world. She kept apologizing for giving me up and she asked for my forgiveness over and over. She explained why it was necessary at that time, and I completely understood. If she had not put me up for adoption, I probably would have died soon afterward. The Lord knew what the future held for all of us and being adopted into the family He gave me was exactly the way it should have been. She told me that she had gone to Charleston, West Virginia when she was only a few months pregnant and worked in a nursing home that belonged to her aunt. Shortly after my birth, she was told by the aunt, that I had died. That is why she didn't realize it was me when we spoke at the funeral home. She thought it was very coincidental that I had the same name she had given me at birth, but she never thought that I could have been alive after believing that I had died. She had never told anyone else of my birth, because of the situation at that time. During that same conversation, we found out that she and I had been saved the same year when I was twelve years of age.

During this past year we have visited as much as possible. I am so close to all of them and we cherish each minute we are together. As I reflect back on my life, I ask, "Why me Lord?" Why did He heal my heart and give me wonderful, Christian parents and most of all, allow me to find my natural family after all those years.

Well, that pretty much completes this story. It has been the most exciting and unbelievable time of my life and my greatest wish is that all who read this, will be truly blessed as I have been to have lived through it.

REMEMBERING THE BRAXTON COUNTY MONSTER
By Dennis Deitz

The date was September 13, 1952, when a landing was made in Flatwoods, West Virginia, of something generally known as The Braxton County Monster. It is locally referred to as the "Green Monster". At each end of the town is a sign which read "Flatwoods, home of the Green Monster."

The landing site was within about a mile of the exact center of the state of West Virginia. The report of this landing created excitement, not only in the state, but also throughout the United States where it was one of the 10 top stories of 1952.

This writer read the many stories that were written in local and national news, but not with any special interest. Then, 40 years later, a special interest was developed when I began to gather and publish stories collected from persons who had personal experiences they couldn't explain such as premonitions, dreams that come true, etc.

I recalled that my mother had been about 50 miles away at Richwood, WV, babysitting my nephew, who was about 5 years old at that time. She called to him to come and see the plane flying overhead (not many planes passed over Richwood at that time). She said, after a second look, "That's not a plane, what is it?" The next day she was reading about the landing at Flatwoods. My nephew still remembers this incident.

BRAXTON MONSTER
Interview with Fred May by Dennis Deitz

This interview was with Fred May, son of Kathleen May Horner. Fred was ten years old at the time of the sighting of the Braxton monster.

Fred agreed the reason they never talked about what they had seen was because of the flack they took from schoolmates until they just tired of hearing about it.

They were never called liars directly, as in those days being called a liar was an insult you defended with fists. Instead, they would only repeat what some adult had said, meaning the six boys and Mrs. May had lied until it got real frustrating.

A couple of years ago when an interview with Fred's mother was printed in the newspaper, an opposite reaction happened which made him feel honored. Many long time fellow workers at Union Carbide in Institute, West Virginia came and asked him to confirm his mother's story. When he did, all their reactions were almost the same, saying, "Freddy, I never really believed the story, but when you say it's true, there is no doubt in my mind. I don't believe you would lie about anything."

Mrs. Horner and Freddy agreed on every detail. They had both seen it together, but Fred and the other five boys had seen the landing of the monster from the Flatwoods Elementary School playground.

He described it as a burning ball of fire coming down through the air and landing in a meadow just out of sight over the top of the hill. Fred, his brother Don, and the other four boys started running up the hill. Passing their home, they called their mother (then Mrs. May) who grabbed a flashlight and went with them. Fred believed that a meteorite had landed and was burning up. They were excited, expecting to see it bum. They were not scared at all - at this point. They were close. It sure wasn't a meteorite, nor a plane. It wasn't burning. It was now dusk. Mrs. May turned on her flashlight and just in front of them was the green monster. The sight scared them and now all seven of them raced off the hill. He said he was still so scared the next day that he was afraid to go out in broad daylight.

Then came investigators, amateurs and newspapermen. They were asked to separate and draw pictures of the monster. Later, they compared their drawings and found they all pretty much agreed. They were amazed when a re-drawing appeared in the newspaper showing the monster with long arms and claw-like hands, because the boys' drawings had shown antennas at the shoulders. This caused him to lose faith in newspapers.

He believes that instead of a monster, he saw a mechanical robot and spaceship controlled by a mother spaceship.

KATHLEEN MAY HORNER
By Bessie Hawkins

Kathy Horner was the main witness to the monster sighting in Braxton county.

Kathy Horner was born in Flatwoods, West Virginia, daughter of Joseph N. and Leotha G. McClung Lemon. She attended Flatwoods Grammar and Sutton High Schools. She is a graduate of Martz's Beauty College, Huntington, WV, with a classroom average of 98. (Grades recorded at State Capitol). She became a member of Summit Rebekah Lodge #2, Sutton, WV in March of 1954, and has been an active member of the IOOF, Rebekah Assembly, Social and Community Activities through these years. She transferred her membership to Queen Rebekah Lodge #121 in October, 1975 when she moved to Pennsboro from Braxton County.

Kathy instituted Iris Rebekah Lodge in Summersville, WV in 1967 with 38 charter members signing the membership role. She was presented a trophy from the Rebekah Assembly and Sovereign Grand Lodge for this outstanding membership achievement.

Kathy was also presented with the Decoration of Chivalry and the Honorable Degree conferred upon her in Charleston, WV, in October, 1966. This is the highest Award ever to be bestowed upon or achieved by any female in the United States or Canada. She was elected to receive this award through her outstanding work and her dedication to the social and civic affairs of both the State and Local level.

She organized a volunteer program in 1954 in Braxton County with the assistance of Local Lodges, churches and business places to render assistance to the widows and low-income residents of the County. They raised their funds by way of bake sales, bazaars, yard sales, soliciting from door to door and many other various ways and means.

She was appointed District Deputy President of District 15 of the Rebekah Assembly of West Virginia in October 1966, serving 3 counties which were comprised of 8 different Lodges. She served in this capacity until October 1968. She was reappointed as a District Deputy President of District #6 for her second term in October 1979. She is a Past Noble Grand of both Summit #2 and Queen #121.

She has served as secretary to the following: 4 years, Flatwoods PTA; 4 years, American Cancer Society (Sutton Unit); 15 years, Summit Rebekah Lodge (Sutton); 11 years, Harold L. Scott Drill Team of WV; 4 years, Recorder for town of Flatwoods; 2 years, queen Rebekah Lodge (Pennsboro, WV); I year, Committee on Aging (Harrisville, WV); present secretary, Foster Grandparent Program; present secretary, District #6 R.A. of WV. serving her 3rd term; 2 years, treasurer C.O.A. (Harrisville, WV); I year, treasurer Ladies Auxiliary F.O.E. #2385 (Pennsboro, WV); 2 years, treasurer American Red Cross (Sutton); 3 years, treasurer Football Mothers (Sutton); I year, treasurer Queen Rebekah Lodge (Pennsboro, WV). Also served I year on the Braxton County High School Committee for the promotion of the County High School.

She instituted Friendly Theta Rho Girls Club, Sutton, WV in April 1954 with 32 charter members. She served as their Advisor until March 1975.

She began her employment with Ritchie County Community Action, Inc. in February 1977 as a Senior Citizen's Aide under the Federal Program. She was then transferred to the Youth Program, March 1978. She served in this position until May of 1978 when she then accepted the office of Senior Citizen's Coordinator. She served in this capacity until March of 1979 when she then was elected by the Ritchie County Board of Directors as Director of Ritchie County C.A.A., the position she now holds.

She organized the Smithville Senior Citizen's Satellite with 48 charter members in July of 1978. July of 1980 she organized the Glendale Senior Citizen's Satellite with 24 charter members. She was presented a certificate for her outstanding achievement and accomplishments in these 2 centers from the Action Program of the Federal Government.

She has served in various offices of the Rebekah Assembly of WV, traveling throughout the United States and Canada. She is a former member of Flatwoods United Methodist Church, a member of the Church Choir, taught the Intermediate class for 15 years and the Junior class for 5 years. She was also Dramatics Director of the church with her name on the Cradle Roll. She is now a member of Pennsboro United Methodist Church.

She was advisory counselor for Youth Camp, Camp Caesar, Webster County which was held the second week in July of each year for 12 consecutive years. These youths were between the ages of 12-18 and came from all over the state of WV.

Kathy is an active member of the following organizations: Queen Rebekah Lodge #121, Pennsboro, WV; Mountain Grange, Mountain, WV; Pamona Grange, State of WV; Harold L. Scott Drill Team, State of WV; Pythian Sisters Temple, Richwood, WV; Professional Business Woman's Assoc., Sutton, WV; American Cancer Society, Sutton, WV; American Red Cross, Sutton, WV; American Legion Auxiliary, Marietta, OH; Glendale Women's Club, Glendale, WV; Mountaineers For Rural Progress, Harrisville, WV; F.O.E. Ladies Auxiliary, Pennsboro, WV; L.A.P.M. Department Assoc' ', Clarksburg, WV; I.A.R.A. Opportunity Club, International; Past Dis't. Deputy Pres. Assoc., State of WV; Secretaries Assoc., State of WV; Modern Woodmen of America, Rock Island, IL; Rebekah Assembly, State of WV; Theta Rho Assembly, State of WV; 35th Star Foundation, Inc., Charleston, WV.

Kathy has also received the following meritorious awards of special recognition: Certificate and gold diamond pin, presented by the Sovereign I.O.O.F. Lodge of the World; (she was the only recipient from the State of WV to receive this honor); Rhinestone lapel pin from the American Cancer Society in recognition of 20 years of dedicated service to society and the community; The A.M. Black Sovereign Grand Masters Certificate Award; The Harold L. Scott Sov. Grand Masters Certificate of Accomplishment; Special 150th Anniversary Award Certificate from Chester J. Hunnicutt; The Ray J. King Special Recognition Award; Jennie Sue Pierson Award of Accomplishment "Special Recognition"; The Shelby McCauley Membership Expansion Award; Myrtle L. Russell pin and certificate; Kathy was elected into the "Order of the Red Rose" and was the only individual from the State of WV to receive this honor. There were only 6 recipients of the United States to receive this honorable distinction. She was promoter of the Football Mothers banquet at Sutton High and served as their Football Mother for 6 years. This is still an annual affair at Sutton. She was also very active with the basketball team and their activities. She transported 5 to 6 of the team members to various events when the school bus couldn't transport them.

She helped to organize the Disaster Center at Chatteroy and Williamson, WV when they experienced the terrible flood of 1977. She worked 14 days (12 hours) per day without a break, processing the victims of this flood by rendering assistance in applying for aid through various agencies from the State, National and local levels. Kathy is still helping and assisting those that need help in any way possible, especially the senior citizens, under privileged, handicapped, and those with low incomes. She spends many hours per day beyond the call of duty.

Her remarks when she returned home from the disastrous flood were, "This is one sad experience I shall never forget. I thank God for the knowledge and talent that he has given me, as it has given me the opportunity and enabled me to serve my fellow man at a very crucial time when needed. I am more thankful now, than ever before, for the possessions that I have at home. This proves that we really do not own anything in this world but our character. When character is destroyed, then we own nothing but a black mark of a disaster and it's remains. We were given life on this earth to help one another and to do unto others as we would have others do unto us. If we would all live by the new commandment that he gave unto us (Love one another as I have loved you) then we would have a much better world to live in, neither would we be breaking any of the other ten commandments. God can wipe out our lives as quickly as he can destroy our earthly possessions. This is why I don't want to stand on dangerous ground and take my God for granted. Life is too precious to waste or throw away."

Kathy is the proud mother of three lovely children; daughter, Valleen Armstrong of Forest Grove, PA; sons, Eddie Don May of Woodbridge, VA who is employed by the C.I.A. and Freddie G. May of Gassaway who is employed by Union Carbide in Institute, WV. She also has 5 grandchildren (2 granddaughters, 3 grandsons), 3 step granddaughters, I step grandson, all of which call her Mamma. Her children give her great praise in the way she raised them from the cradle through. They are as proud of her as we are. She taught them to attend church and to be obedient to God's word.

She has told us many times that she never let a day go by that she didn't thank God for his blessings and to give her the ability to teach and train them in the way he would have them go. I proudly give God the credit for their Christian lives today.

She was elected Queen of Queen Rebekah Lodge #121 in June of 1982 and was presented a beautiful trophy at a very impressive ceremony. We know that she is very worthy of this and all the other awards that have been bestowed upon her. She was also a licensed Insurance Agent and was affiliated with Modern Woodmen of America.

She would never permit any of her family members to be placed in a nursing home. She cared for them in her home until their deaths. Namely: Rev. A.B. McClung, grandfather; Margaret E. McClung, grandmother; Martha J. Riddle, great aunt; William E. Lemon, uncle; Joseph N. Lemon, father; Leotha G. Lemon, mother; Alice V. Lemon, first cousin, 48 years and she

paid for her funeral. She also raised a step daughter from 2 months of age until she was married (Mary I. May), half sister to her children, but younger.

KATHLEEN MAY HORNER AND THE BRAXTON COUNTY MONSTER

I lived in Flatwoods, Braxton County, West Virginia on September 12, 1952 with three children and worked as a beauty operator. It was near dusk. My two sons came running to the house along with four other boys. They had been playing at the grade school playground. They announced they saw something fall from the sky, just over the hill, which they thought might be a meteor. I grabbed a flashlight and ran with them up the hill, followed by their two dogs.

This was strange because the dogs followed the boys everywhere. Within minutes we understood that the dogs knew a lot more than we did.

Suddenly, just over the top of the hill was a craft of some sort which appeared to be hovering just two or three feet above the ground. It was round in shape with lights. I turned on the flashlight. Directly in front of me and to one side of the hovering object was something ever afterward known as "The Braxton County Monster" as well as the "Green Monster."

I seemed frozen to the spot for a few seconds before running or at least long enough that the details of this "monster" left a picture in my mind and memory. The "monster" was 10 or 12 feet. All seven of us ran as fast as we could back down the hill to the house. On the way up the hill I had climbed over a rail fence, and on the way back down the hill I cleared or jumped the fence without touching it.

Afterward, people would ask me how fast I thought I was running. My answer was "I don't know except that I out ran some fast teenage boys." I remember the sickening odor at the site like burnt sulphur. One of the boys got sick and vomited for about 24 hours. Our dog went under the house and refused to come out for a day or two. There was oil on my beauty shop uniform.

I started calling for the sheriff and the National Guard. I had trouble getting them because they were away checking on a similar landing about fifteen miles down Elk River at Frametown. When officials finally arrived, the "monster" and UFO or whatever, was gone. Many people had sighted it leaving. A lot of people had seen it but did not realize what it was.

Things became hectic after that. Newspaper reporters came from what seemed like everywhere. The next morning all seven of us were separated and asked to draw a picture of the monster and describe all that we had seen. Later, the six boys and I discussed what we had drawn and described for the newsmen. We found that our descriptions and drawings all matched each other. The newspaper stories didn't always follow what we had written. People kept coming for interviews. Newsmen, UFOlogists, and people who were just curious.

Two men came and said that they were newsmen from Clarksburg, WV. They asked questions and scraped samples of an oil-like substance from my uniform to analyze. Later, I got a letter from these men saying that they were from the Pentagon and that the flying object belonged to the Armed Forces. I continued to be questioned. I was even flown to New York for a TV interview on a national network

Back in 1952, UFO's were not heard of that much and a lot of people just didn't believe that we had seen anything. This disbelief finally led the six boys to the point that they just wouldn't talk about it until my sons Eddie Don, and Freddy granted interviews. I have always told what I saw when asked about it. I still can't explain what I saw on that September day, but I know what I saw so I am willing to say so.

Fred May was ten years old at the time. He said that when the seven persons were separated and their stories and drawings were alike, it caused him to lose faith in newspapers. He said that although all seven had drawn sketches of the "Green Monster" showing no arms but antennas at the shoulders, the newspapers had the sketches redrawn showing arms.

He has a theory that they hadn't seen a "monster" but a robot controlled through the antennas by a "mother" ship or UFO. Fred grew up, went to school and became an engineer for Union Carbide at Institute, WV. An interesting note is that when an article appeared in the Charleston Metro West, Fred was identified as one of the witnesses to the sighting. Men who had worked with him asked if this was a true story.

All of his fellow workers almost without exception said, "I never quite believed this story, but if you say it's true, I have no more doubts about the story."

Kathleen's other son, Eddie Don May, is one year older than Fred. He was eleven years old at the time of the incident. He grew up, finished school, and went to work for the C.I.A. until retirement.

He added little to the story except to verify everything told by his mother and brother.

INVASION OF THE GREEN MONSTERS

The following version of the Braxton County Monster is from a book "Appalachian Ghost Stories " by James Gay Jones. Many thanks to Mr. Jones for permission to use this story.

Late in the evening of September 13, 1952, a number of unidentified spacecraft passed over the eastern area of the United States. They were moving in a northwest direction and were observed by people in Virginia, Maryland, Pennsylvania, and Ohio, as well as in West Virginia. While passing over the Allegheny Plateau, at least three of the spacecraft became separated from the others, two of which apparently met with disaster in the hills of Clay and Braxton Counties of West Virginia. Whether these were remote control destructions or accidental ones, no one here will ever know; however, a review of the evidence as reported by those who witnessed the strange happenings indicates that both causes may have been involved.

In Clay County, a number of witnesses reported having observed a strange luminous ball passing low overhead in the twilight of the evening. It drifted to a lower elevation and ended in a dazzling flash of light on a wooded hillside. Those who investigated the scene soon afterward reported that the spacecraft, while on the way to obliteration against the hill, had seared a swath of forest foliage crisp and brown, and filled the air thereabouts with a lingering acrid odor.

The incident which received the most widespread publicity was the appearance of the so-called "Braxton County Monster." Mrs. Kathleen May of Flatwoods (a few days after the occurrence) reported to a nationwide television audience that she joined a group of young people to investigate the claim of her two sons that they had seen a flying saucer land on the hillside overlooking the small town. On climbing the hill they "came upon a monster ten feet tall, with a bright green body and a blood-red face" which moved toward them with a sliding, floating motion. A noxious odor filled the area which brought on violent choking spasms and vomiting by some members of the search party as they fled from the scene. Subsequently, investigators reported smelling the sickening odor as well as observing burnt and broken branches of the trees where the flying object had landed, but the monster and its spacecraft had disappeared.

An incident which received little publicity at the time was that observed on the same evening by George Snitowsky and his wife, Edith, of Queens, New York, while they were traveling by car between Frametown and Gassaway, a few, miles to the east of Flatwoods. Without any warning, the motor of their car stopped and a quick check indicated that the practically new battery was dead. They said that suddenly a faintly sickening odor somewhat like a mixture of burnt sulphur and ether filled the air about them and caused their baby to have an attack of coughing and gagging. While Edith attempted to console the child, George went out to try to locate the source of the odor.

Crossing over a slight rise to the left of the highway, he saw, some sixty yards down the slope, a large spheroid moving slowly back and forth as it hovered near the ground and from it came a soft, violet light. On moving closer to the object, he felt the sensation of thousands of needle-like vibrations irritating the skin of his whole body. Nauseated, he turned and stumbled back toward the car.

From the car Edith gave a piercing scream. George could see her ashen face, her trembling lips, and her eyes wide and staring.

"Edith,- for God's sake, what's the matter?" George shouted.

"Hurry, George, hurry," she cried in terror, "It's coming behind you!"

George glanced back over his shoulder and saw, some one's feet behind him, a figure about eight or nine feet tall with a big head, bloated body, and long, spindly arms gliding rapidly toward him. On entering the car he hurriedly rolled up the windows, locked the doors, then dived to the floor under the steering column. Meanwhile, Edith had crouched with the baby to the floor in the back seat of the car where she tried to relieve her child of its gagging and crying by placing a silk handkerchief over its face. Then, terror-stricken, they waited to see what the monster would do.

After some time, George rose up slowly and saw a long, spindly arm, forked into two soft ends, reach across the windshield and touch the hood of the car. After another agonizing wait, he looked again and saw the monster glide across the road and up and over the slope in the direction of its spacecraft. With a feeling of slight relief they watched and waited.

"Then," George related later, "my eye caught sight of the ascending iridescent globe over the trees .... It rose slowly and made intermittent stops, hanging in mid-air for a split second before continuing upward. And then at about three thousand feet, I guess, it swung back and forth like a pendulum gathering momentum. Suddenly it swooped up in an elliptical arc and with a dazzling trail of light, shot completely out of sight."

A half hour later the Snitowskys, pale-faced and still thoroughly shaken from the ordeal, stopped at a motel in Sutton for the night without telling anyone at the time about their terrifying experience. Because of the usual skepticism held by the public toward such phenomena and the accompanying ridicule for those reporting having seen them, they believed it wise, for the time, to remain silent.

The next morning while getting gas at a nearby service station before resuming their trip, the attendant pointed out to Snitowsky a V-shaped brown spot on the hood of his car that appeared to have been burned into the paint. Having heard of the Flatwoods scare of the evening before, the attendant said in mock seriousness, "It looks as if the Green Monster was after you, too."

Looking the attendant directly in the eye, George replied, "I wish you could have seen it."

As the family drove away, the attendant said to his helper, "By golly, he said that as if he really meant it!"

SOMETHING GREEN AND ORANGE
By Dexter Pritt

My name is Dexter Pritt. I live in Lizemore, West Virginia. I was arrested January 25, 1992 for driving on a suspended drivers license. I spent 3 days in the jail at Sutton, WV. I was sentenced to serve 7 more days in the new regional jail in Flatwoods, WV when it was finished and opened in January, 1993.

They took me to the new jail on February 22, 1993, to serve the other 7 days. I was in the back seat of the police car. Snow was on the ground, but the road was clear. About one mile before we got to the jail, something crossed in front of the vehicle causing it to wreck. The driver of this car was an officer working at the jail. No one could explain or describe what had appeared in front of the car causing the wreck.

I was incarcerated in the B.5 section in cell 16. In the same section was a fellow from Webster County named Teny Wood, as well as "Dog" Harvey from Lewis County and Jimmy Stone from Clay County.

The very first night in jail, February 22, 1993, I was looking out the cell window when I saw something drop out of the sky and into the snow. I could see lights from houses on the north side, I think. I could see tracks shaped like dog tracks about 6 inches big around. What I saw drop into the snow was 10 or 12 feet tall. It was green and orange. It slowly changed shape, like a wolf or I thought maybe a werewolf. It continued to change shapes until it resembled a black man. I saw the same thing, a monster, my last night in jail on March 1, 1993.

Whether the other men in my section saw what I saw, I am not sure. I had a feeling from their actions that they were scared by something. After both sightings I felt like my legs and lower body were almost frozen.

The first of the three crosses, by Rev. Coffendaffer, was placed near this spot. Whether there is any connection, I don't know.

Today I still have a feeling of fear if I were to leave Clay or Fayette County. I was advised to carry garlic powder at all times (an old remedy to ward off evil spirits) and I will not be without it.

THE SIGHTING
By Ruth E. Lears

I assume you have been to the area where this was supposed to have occurred but in case you haven't, here is the tale as I originally heard it. Some of it was described in papers and even on a morning TV program from New York.

The houses and hill are alongside a road that was well traveled. The boys were up in the woods or near them and something scared them. They ran down to get Mrs. May (the mother of one or two) and told her to come see. She took a small flashlight and went up the hill, turned the light on to see a large pulsating ball of fire on a space ship. The monster stepped out and then got on the ship and left. They went down to Mr. Edward's home where the details are told on another page.

I found it difficult to believe one would need to use a small flashlight to see a space ship or ball of fire. I don't want to say that the group didn't see anything, but found it impossible to accept the version told by Mrs. May. I did talk to people who were there that confirmed my disbelief.

Dr. J.C. Eakle was called to the home of a Mr. Edwards to check one boy who had hyper-ventilated, and that the Dr. said that he was just scared.

I talked to Mr. Edwards, whose home the boys and Mrs. May went to. He said, "One boy said, 'It's a good thing Mrs. May didn't see what we saw.'"

I talked to Neil Nenly when he was 16 or 17 years old. He was 12 or 13 when 'it' happened, and he said it didn't happen. He was one of the boys.

Some explanations of the things that were supposedly seen.

1. An oil spill from the space ship. (Answer: A farmer had drained his tractor in that area).

2. A foul smelling mist seen in a distance. (Answer: A train had gone through the Morrison Tunnel that was nearby and the steam and smoke came out thicker than the amount seen, just in passing.)

My father and I wrote a letter to the *Charleston Gazette* (published) stating what we believed to be an exaggeration. That's the kindest word I can use as I don't want to say, but we ended the letter saying, "I would like to get a free trip to New York, but would like to go by another means of transportation than on the "Tale of a Monster."

A man from another county put one in that he hoped the next one landed in our backyard and I replied "I hope if one does, it doesn't take one look at me and leave."

It seems that no one else saw this "whatever" and besides the residents, there was usually a lot of traffic on the road. I've tried to separate the things I'm not sure about from the ones that I heard from those who were there. It didn't make sense to me then and it still doesn't. It has been played up and still people seem to believe it, but they are miles away from here. The ones nearby didn't think so, at least many that I talked to.

TRUE GHOST AND OTHER ODD STORIES
By Michelle Henson

I hope you do not think I am insane for telling you what I am about to tell you. Well, I guess I should just tell you flat out that I see things that no one else can see, hear things no one else hears, and dream things that really come true.

I began to realize my gift at age five, when my father died. My mother and I went to his funeral and as we were walking in I noticed this woman in a casket. She sat up and looked at me. Then, she got out of the casket and stared at me. She seemed angry. I looked at my mother, and she could not see the woman. My mother said that I was imagining things. That is when I knew I was different. My mother says sometimes she can still feel my dad standing behind her, so, I guess it just runs in the family.

I am not going to tell you my life story, just the good parts. I will start with my dreams. I have these dreams that predict the future. Usually only the next day, but sometimes I can see for weeks ahead. When my sister got pregnant I was scared for her. One night I dreamt that we were in this building that was about to fall down. She walked into a room with a glass ceiling. I started screaming at her to get out. I did not know why. I was just frightened. She looked up and the ceiling began to break. All the jagged glass came falling towards her. After it all fell I went to help her. I was so scared for her. Then I looked down and the bottom of her stomach in between her pelvic bones was bleeding. The cut was about six inches wide. Somehow her baby was okay. I woke up the next morning, terrified that something was going to happen to her. I did not care if the baby was fine in my dream or not. About three weeks later, my sister went for a checkup. She came home upset. The doctor told her she needed a c-section.

Next comes the chilling part of my story. I can feel them touch me. (The spirits that is.) Sometimes I can not move. It is like I am frozen. I can not speak or hear anything. I am petrified. Sometimes it can be scary, but then it can also be peaceful.

I was at a friend's house and it was about two in the morning. I was getting a glass of water, and as I turned the corner to go to her room I noticed something strange out of the corner of my eye. I looked over, and out the window was a man I had never seen before. That is because he was dead. I do not remember exactly what happened. All I know is that I could not move, speak, blink, or hear anything. After about two minutes I turned around to see my friend yelling at me. She said that she had been yelling at me for forever. I did not realize that I had seen a ghost until about 3 months ago. Two years after it happened I had had a flashback. I described the man to my friend and it was her grandfather. I had described someone I had never even seen a picture of. My friend was crying it scared her so bad.

Another occurrence was at my ex-boyfriends' house about 8 months ago. His dad had passed away in his house the Christmas before, so I was wary of the place. I was sitting in the kitchen alone and I was looking around. I got this chill on my neck, and I felt a hand slide slowly down my back and it lingered for awhile. I turned to find that no one was there.

I am going to tell you about some of the things I have seen. Sometimes the ghosts can scare you. If you are like me you cannot be scared. You have a gift that will be with you for the rest of your life; so, you have to deal with it. The only way you can get rid of it is to shut the door, which can be impossible.

I was coming in the house from school one day. I was walking through the kitchen, when I looked around to see into the den. In the den sat a beautiful angel dressed in a light blue dress with curly, long, blonde hair sitting on the arm of a rocking chair. Her eyes were so blue. She had a peaceful smile. All at once her smile began to fade. She disappeared. I was afraid to go any further because the rocking chair was rocking by itself.

I hear them whispering all the time. I feel like I am going crazy sometimes. This is the only part that really scares me. I will wake up and hear them. I cannot ever understand what they are whispering about. I am glad that I cannot.

Once, I was alone in my room and it was 3:45 a.m. I woke up from dreaming and was really thirsty, but also for some strange reason I was frightened - like something was going to get me. I drank two full glasses of water and tried to sleep. I closed my eyes and a bright luminous light flashed across my eyes. I had just prayed to God to make me feel safe. I opened my eyes and a cross went across my eyes, twice. I was no longer afraid. I went to my mother and she was getting ready for work at four. She just stared at me like she was frozen. Then I went back to bed. Two days later, at 3:45 am, I woke up and saw a bright white skull flash across my eyes. People do not understand that people like me have times during the night, the active time, where we get most of the activity. Houses even have these times during the night. So, if there is anything you are afraid of about ghosts, take it from me, you have no idea.

Thank you. Be careful, but not afraid.

GHOSTBUSTING
By Juanita Teeters

My name is Juanita Teeters. I am a sensitive. I have worked with ghostbusting. I started working with the Athens state foundation in Athens, AL. We formed a group under the direction of Joe Slate. One of the calls that we received was to a brand new office building in Alabama. They were having sightings and were having things happen. 911 calls were being made from their office at night when no one was there. Electrical outlets were taken off the wall. Papers were jumbled. We went in and with a table tilting technique, we were able to communicate with the entity that was there. Through communication by the table we were able to determine that he was a real Indian scout from the Civil War. He was scouting for the confederate soldiers. We found out from him that a terrific battle had occurred there in Madison on the particular property where this building had been built and located. At the end of the battle, several were killed. He was badly wounded and they left him behind. He expressed terrific anger at being left. When we talked to him about leaving and going to the light, he refused and demonstrated his anger through the table. We started to negotiate with him that he could stay there as long as he did not play anymore bad tricks, like dialing and inconveniencing the 911 operators, and that he lived in peace with the people who were there. As far as we know, it is still peaceful. The last time that we checked with him, he was still there and was happy with the arrangement. The people were very happy also.

Another time, we were contacted by a friend of the family, a young couple who lived in Huntsville, AL. They had a nine month old baby. They told us that one of the occurrences that they were concerned about was that every night at eleven fifteen someone, or something would let the rail down on the baby's crib and they could see the rocker in the room moving. This entity would also move the pictures in the baby's room by putting their faces toward the wall. They called us and asked us if we could help. After they made the call, and before we arrived at the house, the father of the young baby had holes stabbed in his new jeans all up and down the legs. After we arrived, again using the table to communicate, we found out that it was a young woman in her 20s who had died in a car wreck. She had left behind a young baby that she was worried about, and she didn't know where it was. Since this house was near the wreck sight, she picked it because she found another baby there. She informed us that she was protecting and caring for the baby so that nothing would ever happen to it. We told her that she was not needed there to care for the baby because it had a mommy and daddy. Her family was waiting for her on the other side. We asked her if we directed her to the light would she be willing to go and she said yes. We did a prayer and showed her the way to the light. We could feel her energy moving in the direction of the light. The house was peaceful and the baby never had any more visitors.

We had a very diverse group of people who worked with us. When we worked as a group to help those with spirit problems, our size varied with how many people were available at the time. My daughter and myself and another sensitive that is still working in Alabama were the three main ones. We would bring in more people as we needed them. Especially with the Indian. We added a larger number to improve our effectiveness.

... AND THERE I WAS AT TWENTY THOUSAND FEET...!!!

By Robert Evans

At about 3:00 PM. and approximately 20,000 feet of rapidly diminishing altitude over Tokyo, Staff Sgt. Robert Paul Evans reached for his ripcord.

Just sixty seconds earlier and 29,000 feet above Tokyo, Japan, Robert Evans had been performing his duties as a flight radar operator assigned to the 881st Squadron of the 500th B-29 Bomb Group, United States Army Air Force. It was a routine air raid consisting of a hundred and fifty B-29 Superfortresses, three of which were destroyed, including the one in which Robert served as radar operator.

Seven and one-half hours earlier and fifteen hundred miles to the south they had lifted off from their operations base in Saipan. It was Robert Evans' ninth mission of the thirty-five required of each crew member.

A twin-engined enemy fighter plane had been terminally damaged by the guns of a Superfortress in an adjacent flight element. As witnessed by crew from another B-29 flying some 500 feet above Robert's plane, the Japanese pilot rammed his crippled bird into the spine of the bomber in which Robert rode. The explosive impact broke the Superfortress in two.

Robert had been miraculously blown out of and away from the back half of his B-29. After falling for the better part of a minute from an initial altitude of 29,000 feet to a level he later estimated to be 20,000 feet, Robert regained consciousness. He then managed to deploy his parachute, even as the burning pieces of his B-29 Superfortress continued to fall earthward beneath him.

After parachuting safely to earth in mountains some 30 miles west of Tokyo, Robert was greeted by the standard welcoming committee for uninvited and hostile foreigners. He was promptly escorted to a 'Rising Sun Guest Center' where he would be detained in minimal comfort until the end of the war. The date was February 14, 1945, the same day American marines had captured the beaches of Iwo Jima seven hundred miles to the south of Tokyo.

The records indicated only Robert Evans survived from the entire crew of eleven, even though six parachutes were seen to open. At the first compound where Robert was imprisoned, he recognized the voice and name of one fellow crew mate who died soon after from serious burns and lack of medical care.

Following is Robert's own account of an unusually clear transcendental type experience relating directly to his concern for his parents:

"I had been in the Japanese prison camp for several months in a very small cell. I had two cell mates, an interned Japanese Episcopal minister and a Japanese communist sympathizer. It was very cramped.

When not lying down or standing we stayed in a cramped, kneeling position. The Episcopal minister, Reverend Peter Shukatana, who had preached against the war, often reminded me he was praying for my safety.

I never really worried about myself. I was thinking of my parents back home and worrying about them. I sometimes think that had a lot to do with me staying alive. My mother had a bad heart. I knew that she wouldn't know whether I was dead or alive. Would this kill her? And my father... her death might kill him.

When in that cramped, kneeling position there were many times I would force everything out of my mind and see only the faces of my mother and father. I would concentrate only on the thought of them and not allow any other thoughts to intrude. At the same time I would pray for their well-being and for them to know I was okay and would come home okay.

When the war was over I came home and they told me this strange story:

At the time I was in prison worrying about them, they both had dreams about me the same night. My father said, "I had a dream about Robert last night," and my mother said, "So did I, what did you dream?" Dad said, "tell yours first." Then she said, "I saw him in a very cramped position on his knees." Then my father said, "I had the same dream." As near as we could figure out all three incidents took place at the exact same time.

Shortly thereafter, my sister returned home from a funeral where she had overheard people (who were not aware she was sitting directly behind them) saying Robert was definitely dead. My mother assured her that I was alive and would absolutely return alive and well and had no doubt about it.

From that moment on, after her dream about me, my mother never doubted that I would be home alive, even though everyone else in my home believed I had died when my plane was blown out of the sky."

GRANDMA'S HOUSE
by Joel Neace

My mother, Margaret Neace, was a loving and devoted mother who loved her children and grandchildren, and showed it every day.

After her death, my wife and I drove home to Chauncey, WV for a week. We stayed at my mother's house with my brother James.

As we sat in the living room, we noticed the cords to the curtain blinds were swinging back and forth. The cord suddenly hit against the wall. I remembered how my mother would sit by the window and curl her toes around the cords and swing them back and forth.

Later, my nephew, Donnie, drove down and decided to spend the night. We sat up talking until very late that night. I told him to choose a bed, and he chose my mother's feather bed.

After a while, I heard a commotion coming from the room and I went to check on him. He looked up and said, "I'm ok. It was only Grandma. She was covering me up."

After that, my son Joel and his wife were sitting on the couch and we were all watching TV together. I went on to bed, and 10 minutes later, Joel called out and came up the hallway.

"Dad," he began, "I saw a hand come over me and stroke my hair!" He was shaking and stuttering out his words.

I told him that was just his Grandmother. It scared him so badly that he still won't talk about it today.

Many strange things have happened in the house since my mother passed away, but I don't have any fear about it. I know it's just her - keeping a watchful eye out for her family.

FREDDIE
by Sandy Colegrove

My husband, Freddie Colegrove, was diagnosed with terminal cancer. I could not accept the fact that I was losing him. It was the darkest period of my life, and I thought I'd never cope with his pending death.

During the months that followed, a series of strange and unexplainable things occured that gave me more insight into death, and I am convinced that there is a realm of the spiritual world that transcends our ability to comprehend.

Freddie and I had been married for 27 years, and although he was 20 years older, the age difference was never a problem. Freddie was the love of my life, and I adored him.

I would watch him from a distance as he stood on the porch smoking and taking in the view around him, and I break down and cry and then I would get angry.

"Freddie, don't you know what you're doing to yourself? You have lung cancer! Don't you know that you are dying and you're going to leave me soon enough?"

"Now, Sandy," he would say calmly. "Death is just a part of living. You're young, and you've got your whole life ahead of you. You have to go on. Don't you be worrying about me."

I look back now and think about the many times he said that to me and to my family. "Sandy's young. She has to go on."

The end came too soon, and I found myself amazingly calm at the hospital, along with my son, Tommy Joe, and his wife, Melanie, watching helplessly as the life support was removed and I watched him slip away from me forever.

I bent down and whispered in his ear, "Freddie, honey, I've gone as far as I can go. You'll have to go on without me from here. Twenty years may be a long time for me. It will pass just like the blinking of an eye, and I promise you, honey, that I will find you wherever you are. In the meantime, if there's some way you can show me that you're okay, then I'll be okay. I always loved you, and I always will." I kissed him softly and watched as he took his last breath.

I was amazed at the calmness I felt. I suppose I had grieved so much over the past 2 years of his illness that I had conditioned myself for the inevitable, and I felt a peace.

We left the hospital in the new Jeep we had just bought. Tommy Joe was driving with Melanie seated beside him in the passenger seat up front, while I sat in the back. Melanie and Tommy Joe reached back and patted me on the knee to console me when all of a sudden my window rolled down. I never thought anything of it, but said, "Are you getting warm, Melanie?"

Melanie looked puzzled. "I never rolled the window down. There's no control for the back windows on my side, only a control for my window."

I looked at Tommy Joe. I knew he hadn't rolled down the window because he was driving with one hand and patting me on the knee with the other. I knew I hadn't rolled it down. I was seated in the middle of the seat and couldn't have accidentally bumped the control. Then I thought of what I had just told Freddie, and I remembered the little game he use to play with me every time I fell asleep in the car. He would roll down my window and the wind in my face would wake me suddenly. He would laugh and I would fuss. That gave me comfort, for it was as if he was letting me know he was okay. That helped me to get through the agony of the funeral.

Two weeks after Freddie's death, my mother called. She knew how depressed I was, and she tried to help. "Sandy, I'm coming to pick you up, so you be ready. We're going to Charleston." I really welcomed her visits. I needed her strength, and her love, and she always had a way of lifting my spirits. I told her I would be ready.

A short while later, the phone rang, and I noticed on the caller ID that it was my friend, Lil. I knew if I got on the phone with her that I wouldn't be ready when my mother came, so I decided I'd call her back when we returned. I finished getting dressed and my mother still hadn't come, and I noticed the light flashing on the caller ID and realized that Lil had probably left a message, so I listened.

"Where the h— are you?" she began.

"Am I crazy or what?" I asked myself. "Was that what I thought it was?" I played the message again, and just as before, in the background I distinctly heard a man's voice and it was saying, "Don't grieve for the dead, for the Bible says to go on..." (Lil is now speaking)..."You're young, you're young, you're young."

My mother had now arrived, and I ran to the car and said, "Come in here and listen to this and tell me if I am crazy or what!"

She listened and stared at me in amazement. She heard it, too.

I then remembered the book I had read and tossed aside. That's exactly what Freddie had always told me, "You're young, you're young."

I called my friend, Lil, and asked if anyone was with her when she had made that call, and she said she had been alone.

In the 27 years we were married, Freddie was always in my dreams. They were happy, joyful dreams, and were always pleasant to remember.

Suddenly, the dreams stopped. I dreamed as usual, but Freddie was no longer in my dreams, and I longed to see him again, if only in my dreams.

One night, six weeks after Freddie's death, I had a dream and Freddie was in it, but it was nothing like the dreams I had had before. In the dream, I was standing beside his casket, and they opened it and inside I saw Freddie. He was slumped down, but still in the same position he was in at the funeral. His skin was dark and decaying, and I noticed his teeth were exposed more. I woke up suddenly and gasped.

Why would I dream such a thing?" I asked my mother. "It was so awful seeing him that way. I don't understand."

It wasn't until 2002 that I understood the meaning of the dream. I had gone to the mausoleum where Freddie was entombed, and noticed he was no longer there in the spot he had originally been in. He had been moved several rows down. I hadn't given orders for his body to be moved, so I couldn't understand why they had moved him.

I called the cemetery as soon as I got home to inquire about their reason for moving him.

"Oh, he hasn't been moved, Mrs. Colegrove," they assured me.

"But I assure you he has been moved," I replied. "I just left the cemetery, and Freddie was beside Dr. Cudden before, and now he is 6 - 8 rows down from there."

They told me they would call back.

"Mrs. Colegrove," she began. "You're husband has been moved back," she confirmed. He's beside Dr. Cudden again."

"But that doesn't answer my question," I started. "I want to know why he was moved. I won't know if he's really there or several rows down. I won't know which place to decorate."

"Mrs. Colegrove," she interrupted, "would you recognize his casket if you saw it again?"

"Sure, I'd recognize it," I assured her.

We agreed to meet at the mausoleum.

Freddie's son, Lee, from a former marriage, went along, as well as my mother. When the lid was opened, Lee nodded his head to confirm that that was his father, then added, "Don't come around here, Sandy."

My mother spoke up and said, "Sandy, this will be the last time you'll get to see him. Do you want to?"

The owner of the cemetery asked, "Do you think you're up to this?"

I smiled, remembering my dream, and told her,"I've already seen him."

I walked around the casket and gazed down to the still form before me, and Freddie was just as I had seen him in my dream.

I will always believe that I had that dream to prepare me for that day.

Although it might seem a little soon to some, I began dating 6 months after Freddie's death. I missed him so much, and Larry helped to fill the void left in my world when I lost Freddie.

One day, we were talking and laying across the foot of my son's bed. It was across from his closet. Larry looked over at me and asked, "Do you think you will ever love me as you did Freddie?"

All of a sudden, it sounded like a bowling ball fell inside the closet. We both sat up and looked in the direction of the crash. I jumped to my feet and opened the closet door, and to my surprise, nothing was out of place, and nothing was on the floor. I looked at Larry and he said, "What the..."

"Apparently, Freddie Colegrove didn't like what you just asked me," I said.

Larry lives on a farm, and I often go there. I take Freddie's two little dogs with me when I go, so Larry built a pen for them.

One day we decided to go horseback riding, and Larry got my horse ready, but it was fussing and carrying on so that I was afraid to mount it, so I asked Larry if he could do something.

He mounted the horse and took off down the hill, and soon, the horse calmed down. I smiled as I watched him, and I thought about Larry's mother, Peggy, who had also passed away, and I said aloud, "Peggy, just look at your wild child. I'll tell you what. I'll take care of him for you if you'll say hello to Freddie for me."

That night as I was sleeping, I had the most incredible experience. It wasn't like a dream. It was more like what people would describe as a vision. The details were so much more vivid.

There in the pen that Larry had built for Freddie's dogs stood Freddie. He was wearing a burgundy shirt and black dress pants with a black belt that had a gold buckle. His fingers were tucked inside his pants pockets and I noticed the thickness of his hands, and I studied his face. He was grinning.

I smiled as I approached him. I had always wondered what it would be like to see him again, and there he was.

"How are you doing, Sandy?" he asked. I smiled and said, "I'm doing just fine. How are you?"

"I'm okay," he replied, and then vanished.

I can still see his image before me. He seemed happy and at peace, and I am at peace with his death. I will always love him and miss him, and someday, I will keep my promise to him that I made that night in the hospital.

"Wherever you are, Freddie, someday I will find you."

SAMSON
by Don Vance

A young man stood in our congregation, and said he had an experience he wanted to share. On his way to church that night, he was following behind another car when the driver suddenly lost control and went over an embankment and the car lodged up against a tree.

He pulled off the road and ran to help.

The man was pinned inside the vehicle. The dash had been moved forward from the impact, and the steering wheel was pressed against his chest.

"All I could think of was to pray," he continued. "I said, 'God, give me the strength of Samson,' as I tried to move the steering wheel back to free the man. I pushed and shoved and prayed, but nothing happened."

Frustrated, he told the man he would be right back, then ran to his car and called for help, all the while wondering why God had not answered his prayer.

He remembered he had a jack in the trunk, so he hurriedly retreived it and ran back down the hill. He managed to brace the jack against the dash and the seat and with every click of the jack the dash moved back until the steering wheel moved enough that he was finally able to free the man from the car. Paramedics arrived and took over.

The young man stayed at the scene long enough to make sure the man would be alright, and then took the jack back to his trunk before continuing on to church.

All the while, he questioned God. "Why did you not answer me when I needed you? I don't understand."

As he placed the jack in the trunk, he noticed the name brand: SAMSON.

GRANDMOTHER'S PERCEPTIONS
by Margie Pullen

My grandparents were John and Julia Ann (O'Keeffe) Rostron. My grandfather was from Bolton, England, the same town where Arthur Rostron, Captain of the ship, "Carpathia", was from. Captain Rostron was credited with rescuing the survivors of the ill-fated Titanic. I never knew whether Captain Rostron and my grandfather were related.

My grandmother seemed to have a sixth sense from a very early age that forewarned her of things to come.

When she was very young, she had a premonition that her god mother was very ill. She was very troubled about the feelings that seemed to overwhelm her. She later learned that while on a voyage to America, her godmother had died and was buried at sea. Her personal belongings were sent to my grandmother.

Call it perception if you like, but my grandmother had the ability to see beyond the realm of our understanding, for prior to leaving for America, she reported seeing her mother standing at the foot of her bed saying, "I'm sick. You need to come." She left promptly and upon arriving at her mother's house, found that she had had a stroke.

In the early 1920's, my grandparents settled in Minden, WV, a small coal mining town that employed more than a thousand miners at one time. There they met and intermingled with other families who had also immigrated from England.

On the main street in town was a family by the last name of Oxendale. They had a daughter who was crippled, and as a child I can remember seeing her sitting on the front porch many times in a wheelchair. Her name was Florence.

I was told that as a child, Florence's mother couldn't stand to hear her daughter's cries from the painful therapy she was required to give her, so she never continued the therapy, and as a result, Florence was never able to walk.

Years later, following the death of my grandfather, my grandmother moved in with Florence for a short period of time. Florence was now living with her sister. They had had a close and lasting friendship that spanned decades. My grandmother was in her 70's at this time, and Florence was still unable to walk.

My grandmother later went to live with my mother and spent the remainder of her years there. I don't recall how long a period of time passed since Florence and my grandmother had seen each other, but one night my grandmother had a dream that Florence had come to visit. She was wearing a yellow dress and she walked down the sidewalk to see her. A few days later, there was Florence in her yellow dress, and she was walking after all those years.

The gift of clairvoyance she seemed to have was with her throughout her life. There were many incidenced, too numerous for me to mention or remember, but these stand out most in my mind.

GRANDMOTHER'S ROLE
by Mike King

I was about 3 years old at the time, but I vividly remember this as if it were yesterday. I was sitting in the living room on the floor playing with the pieces of a Scrabble game.

I could see my grandmother, mother and aunt were busily working in the kitchen. I got up to go to the bathroom, and when I came out, I saw my grandfather lying on the bed.

My grandfather had passed away the year before after battling colon cancer for some time. I was too young to question or reason. I just accepted the fact that he was gone.

He was lying on his side, dressed in a flannel shirt and kakai pants. His arm was propping his head, and he was looking at me. I went to the bed and climbed up and sat down beside him. We began talking.

I had always called him "Sores". He was very sick when I was old enough to romp, so whenever I got close to him, he was afraid I would hurt him and he would touch his stomach and say, "No. Sore."

He said, "Sore's stomach doesn't hurt anymore." He asked me what I had been doing and if I had been good. He told me to always be good to my mother and a good boy.

I suddenly remembered my Scrabble game pieces on the living room floor, so I scooted off the bed and dropped to the floor and told him I wanted to show them to him and I would be right back. I hurriedly ran to the living room and gathered the pieces and ran back, but he was gone.

I went to the kitchen and told my mother. There was quite a commotion in the kitchen that day. Everyone questioned me, but my story never changed. I knew what I had seen and heard.

When I was older, my mother often told me how my grandmother always laid in the floor in front of the fireplace to keep warm. She often talked about how my grandfather would always tuck her robe in around her feet to make sure they didn't get cold, and how my grandmother missed that now that he was gone.

The bathroom at our house was very small, with barely any space between the tub, basin and commode, so it was hard to understand how my grandmother managed to fall into the bathtub after she fainted one day, but there she was in her robe in the bathtub. Her head was underneath the faucets, and her body was stretched out with her feet tucked neatly inside the robe, just like my grandfather always tucked them.

Some things are hard to understand, and now that I am older, I often question the paranormal, but I will never forget the experiences that happened to me as a child. I still cannot explain them. I just accept them.

THE BUS
by Charlotte Vance

"God works in mysterious ways, His wonders to perform." I have heard that scripture all my life, but I saw it in action a few years ago.

Throughout my years of singing gospel music with our family group, The Comptons, we have traveled great distances to sing at churches, concerts, and special events. We always felt God's hand of protection over us, but one incident in particular stands out in my mind.

We were scheduled to sing at two churches in the North Myrtle Beach area of North Carolina. A friend, Lois Barker, worked for a hotel on the beachfront. Her husband was a member of one of the churches where we were scheduled to sing, and Lois had arranged for us to stay at the hotel, and had also made arrangements with the city for us to park our tour bus in a triangular space close by that was formed where 3 streets intersected.

Fortunately, we decided to leave early for the first service. My husband, Don, was our driver. When he got behind the wheel to pull out, the tires began spinning, and the back tires of the bus sank to the bumper in the sand. He and the other men in the group tried in vain to free the tires from the sand before deciding to call for a wrecker.

Don called all over town in vain. Once they heard it was a bus we were driving, no one would come to help. They all said they wouldn't risk tearing up their equipment.

Out of nowhere, a car drove up. Inside were 2 men we had never seen before. They asked us what the problem was, and when we explained, they said they would be back. They said they thought they knew someone with a wrecker that would help.

Time passed, and we were beginning to think they weren't coming back when they pulled up. They told us a wrecker was on the way.

The driver of the wrecker got out and assessed the situation and told us he, too, was afraid of tearing up his equipment, but offered to at least give it a try. He attached the steel cable to the bus and slowly winched it from the sand.

Don stepped inside the bus to get the money to pay the wrecker service, but when he offered the money to them, the two men who had gone for help said, "That's okay. It's been taken care of." They had paid the bill themselves. Don offered the money to them, but they refused to take it.

They said they just wanted to help us.

We invited them to go with us to church and told them where we were singing and also told them the location of the other church we were scheduled at and invited them to come.

We thanked them and told them we had to get on the road or we would be late for the service. When we looked back, Lois Barker was still talking with them.

Three weeks later, we talked with Lois about the two men, and she told me she had gotten their names and addresses and had sent them both a "thank you" card, but the cards both came back marked, "Return to Sender" There was no such person or address.

Other books by Dennis Deitz:

The Greenbrier Ghost Volume 1	$9.95	_____
The Greenbrier Ghost Volume 2	$9.95	_____
Buffalo Creek: Valley of Death	$20.00	_____
Mountain Memories Volume 1	$6.95	_____
Mountain Memories Volume 2	$6.95	_____
Mountain Memories Volume 3	$6.95	_____
Mountain Memories Volume 4	$6.95	_____
Mountain Memories Volume 5	$6.95	_____
A Promise Kept	$6.95	_____
Search For Emily	$4.95	_____
Little Spooner Who Would Not Spoon	$4.95	_____
Man Who Saved 42 Lives: Layland Mine Explosion	$2.95	_____
Molly's Story audio cassette	$3.95	_____
Search For Emily double audio casette	$2.95	_____
Haunting In The Graveyard	$1.00	_____

Prices and availability subject to change.

Send orders to: Pictorial Histories Distribution
                1416 Quarrier Street
                Charleston, WV 25301

Make checks payable to Pictorial Histories.

Please add $3.50 for shipping, and include 6 % sales tax if ordering from West Virginia.

We also take phone orders weekdays from 10-5, and accept Visa/MC. (304) 342-1848 or 888-982-7472.